Trailer

Once inside the trailer, Aga... the scene. "I can see why Trey never leaves this place. There's a fridge, TV, DVD player, CD player, a comfy couch, AC, of course, computer."

"And evidence," Orville put in.

"Yes," Agatha agreed. "Somewhere in this place there has to be evidence that Trey is a robber." Agatha promised herself that all Trey's fans would soon know what kind of person he really was.

Sneaky. Stupid. Slimy. And slippery.

She began patting down the sofa cushions, feeling around for something diamond-ish. Then she checked out the stack of magazines on the end table. No jewelry-size lumps anywhere.

"Everything in here appears normal," Orville reported. "Although there was an unusually large amount of cheese in the refrigerator."

Agatha got down on her hands and knees to inspect the floor when a metallic clang started her heart racing. Someone was on the stairs!

"Someone's coming!" she whispered.

Agatha scanned the trailer for an escape route. Only one door. And three windows. But three windows that didn't open.

They were so totally trapped!

The **Wright &**
Wong Mysteries

Wright & Wong

The Case of the Slippery Soap Star

Laura J. Burns & Melinda Metz

SLEUTH
RAZORBILL

Wright & Wong 4: The Case of the Slippery Soap Star

RAZORBILL

Published by the Penguin Group
Penguin Young Readers Group
345 Hudson Street, New York, New York 10014, U.S.A.
Penguin Group (USA) Inc., 375 Hudson Street, New York, New York 10014, U.S.A.
Penguin Group (Canada), 90 Eglinton Avenue, Suite 700, Toronto, Ontario, Canada M4P 2Y3
(a division of Pearson Penguin Canada Inc.)
Penguin Books Ltd, 80 Strand, London WC2R 0RL, England
Penguin Ireland, 25 St Stephen's Green, Dublin 2, Ireland (a division of Penguin Books Ltd)
Penguin Group (Australia), 250 Camberwell Road, Camberwell, Victoria 3124, Australia
(a division of Pearson Australia Group Pty Ltd)
Penguin Books India Pvt Ltd, 11 Community Centre, Panchsheel Park,
New Delhi - 110 017, India
Penguin Group (NZ), Cnr Airborne and Rosedale Roads, Albany, Auckland 1310,
New Zealand (a division of Pearson New Zealand Ltd)
Penguin Books (South Africa) (Pty) Ltd, 24 Sturdee Avenue, Rosebank,
Johannesburg 2196, South Africa

Penguin Books Ltd, Registered Offices: 80 Strand, London WC2R 0RL, England

10 9 8 7 6 5 4 3 2 1

Interior design by Christopher Grassi

Library of Congress Cataloging-in-Publication Data

Burns, Laura J.
  The case of the slippery soap star / Laura J. Burns & Melinda Metz.
    p. cm. — (Wright & Wong ; 44)
  Summary: When his mother is accused of stealing jewelry at a charity dinner, Orville and
Agatha team up to find the real thief—and their prime suspect is a famous soap opera actor.
  ISBN 1-59514-017-4 (alk. paper)
  [1. Actors and actresses—Fiction. 2. Stealing—Fiction. 3. Soap operas—Fiction.
4. Asperger's syndrome—Fiction. 5. Mystery and detective stories.] I. Metz, Melinda.
II. Title.

PZ7.B937367Cass 2006
[Fic]—dc22

2005023811

Printed in the United States of America

Chapter 1

"I want them to kill Bradford Cadbury." Mrs. Wright's blue eyes gleamed as she spoke. "And I want them to make it hurt. He deserves it for having Melanie sent to prison in his place." Orville's mother checked her lipstick in the car's rearview mirror and gave a satisfied nod.

Agatha Wong didn't care if Brian Cadbury got killed—and couldn't care less about his stupid show, *The Cadburys*.

Nope. Brian, Bradford, Bobo—whatever his name was. Agatha was far more interested in whether Mrs. Wright would agree to lend her that lipstick she was wearing. Because now that she thought about it, Agatha was sure that every female over five at the Placid party would be wearing lipstick. Every female—except her.

"Orville," she whispered to her best friend. "Does your mom consider lipstick sacred, or do you think she would let me have a coat? Make that two coats—one now and one later—'cause I know I can't make it through dinner without some wipeage."

Orville stared at her. Then he turned his attention to his mother. "Sorry, Mom. It is unlikely they will kill Bradford Cadbury."

Agatha gaped at her best friend. Was he ignoring all four-foot nine inches and eighty-eight pounds of her—while she was sitting right next to him in the backseat?

The nerve!

Had she not saved Orville's butt from assorted school bullies—bullies usually named Stu Frysley—since they'd met in the second grade? Had she not explained Orville's "condition" to the popular kids so that Orville could score some ultra-cool friends?

She certainly had, and she deserved better treatment than this!

Agatha stared death rays at her friend's calm, freckled face. But her anger didn't last long.

Orville could be ignoring me because he has no "data" about how protective his mother is of her lipstick, Agatha realized. In Orville's world, and in his giant mega-brain, a lack of data would make the question unanswerable. Which was why . . . well, why Orville didn't answer.

"If they kill Bradford, then Vanessa will never find out that he's not really her father," Orville added.

"True," Mrs. Wright agreed. "Killing Bradford would ruin a good storyline." She sighed. "I don't know why the people who run *The Cadburys* decided to kill off one of the Cadbury men. They should have come up with a better way to boost ratings."

"Will there be anyone at this party who doesn't watch

The Cadburys?" Orville's dad asked from the front passenger seat. "Will anyone be willing to talk about anything besides which character is going to get killed off?"

Agatha raised her hand. "I will, Mr. Wright!"

Half of Agatha's huge extended family watched *The Cadburys* as devotedly as Orville and his mother, but Agatha found the soap opera that was her own life more interesting.

And if Agatha didn't like the show, it was hard to believe Orville found it worth watching for a second. *The Cadburys* was all about emotion, and emotion was something Orville had trouble wrapping his noggin around. Hate, love, jealousy, and all those other soap staples were like a foreign language to him—because of his Asperger's syndrome.

Agatha knew that, because she was Orville's number-one emotion-to-logic translator, just the way Orville translated math mumbo jumbo for her.

Agatha figured watching *The Cadburys* was a lot more about Orville keeping his routine, well, routine. He'd been viewing the show with his mom since he was pre-verbal and unable to protest. And once Orville had a habit, there was no way to break him of it.

"Of course there will be other topics of conversation," Mrs. Wright assured Orville's dad. "The people of Placid are very cultured. I'm sure they'll be happy to discuss art or music or the theater." Mrs. Wright held up one finger. "But remember, theater does not include your swimming pig show at The Grotto, so please don't bring it up."

Whoa. Agatha didn't know what Mr. Wright was going to talk about if he couldn't say anything pig-related. Most of the words she'd traded with him over the years had something to do with Esther and Jeremy—the synchronized swimming pigs who were famous in Agatha and Orville's hometown.

Mr. Wright trained the pigs for the viewing pleasure of diners at The Grotto—the most popular restaurant in Bottomless Lake, Arizona.

"I don't know. I think Mrs. Doheny might like a demonstration of Mr. Wright's hog calls," Agatha teased. "The Squealer and the Grunter are both amazing."

Mrs. Wright didn't laugh. She didn't even smile. Agatha's heart sank. She got the feeling that she'd just lost any chance of securing some lipstick. She also got the feeling that Mrs. Wright was now wishing somebody besides Bradford Cadbury would have to endure a painful death. Somebody named Agatha Hortense Wong.

As if having the middle name Hortense wasn't torture enough.

"Prudence Doheny, president of the Placid Township League of Women Voters, chair of Placid's garden club, and co-chair of Placid's Cheerful Community committee, would not want to hear the collection of . . . of . . .

sounds my husband uses to communicate with pigs," Mrs. Wright said.

"No one in this car will make any animal noises of any kind," Mr. Wright promised. He turned in his seat to give Agatha and Orville an I-mean-business look. "We all know how important this night is to you."

And Agatha did know. Big time.

The Placid Cheerful Community committee didn't usually accept members from poor, neighboring Bottomless Lake, but somehow Mrs. Wright had managed to get invited—after four years of trying. Six months ago, when the group had given Mrs. Wright the job of organizing tonight's party, she had been thrilled!

At the same time, in Agatha's opinion, she also came down with a raging case of the cuckoos. For months afterward, every unoccupied surface of the Wright house had been covered with *party* phone trees and *party* seating charts and *party* expense forms and *party* guest lists.

Mrs. Wright herself was a bundle of nerves, ready to explode over the slightest snag in her party plan. As she reminded everyone within earshot daily, everything about the event had to be perfect.

"Don't worry. The party's going to be fabtastic," Agatha said, trying to make up for her joke bomb. "I don't even watch *The Cadburys* and I'm raring to meet Trey Beck. According to my cousin Serena, he's the most scorching candy bar in the store."

Mrs. Wright glanced in the rearview mirror and blinked at Agatha in an extremely Orville-esque way. Agatha figured an explanation was called for.

"Cadbury. It's a kind of candy bar." Agatha hesitated, trying to decide if more translation was necessary. "And scorching means, you know, um, cute."

Mrs. Wright blinked again.

Agatha sighed. Why didn't anyone understand her? What was she speaking? Martian?

"Trey Beck is the cutest actor who plays one of the Cadburys," she stated. "I will enjoy having the chance to view him up close at the party."

Mrs. Wright nodded, finally figuring it out. "It was very generous of Trey to agree to host the fund-raiser. All the Cadbury actors are in town for a week as part of the show's nationwide tour, but Trey was the only one who agreed to attend. He'd better not be the one they kill as part of their silly advertising campaign. There will be consequences if they try it."

Agatha figured the consequences would probably take the form of a save-Trey letter-writing campaign. But Mrs. Wright spat out the threat, making it sound like dental drills, new shoes with pointy toes, Stu Frysley breath, and other horrible, pain-inducing things.

The road under the small car's wheels smoothed out as it crossed from Bottomless Lake into Placid, the town created and paid for by billionaire Albert L.

Placid. Mr. Moneypants wanted to live in the most perfect place on earth—so he'd built it himself. In Placid, all the lawns were square and green, all the roads were pothole free, and all the citizens looked like they'd slid off a perfect-people conveyor belt. Mrs. Wright was dying to live there. She already worked there, selling real estate.

Orville grooved on the extreme orderliness of the place, but it gave Agatha the wiggins. Sure, Placid was pretty, but it had no personality.

Mrs. Wright turned left onto Succulent Squash Lane—the Placid streets, besides being in alphabetical order, were all named after things beloved by Albert L. Then she made a left into the parking lot of the Albert L. Placid Recreational Center.

Agatha rolled her eyes. Everything in this town not named after something the billionaire liked was named after the billionaire himself.

"Kids! Kids! Trey Beck is here!" Mrs. Wright squealed, her face lit up with excitement. After a moment, her expression faded. "Wait a minute. This is horrible! No one was here to greet him. What must he think of us?" She threw the car into park and leapt out without a backward glance. Agatha watched her clack-clacking across the pavement on her high heels. So much for the borrowing of lipstick.

"Um, I guess I'll just find a spot." Mr. Wright moved

into the driver's seat and pulled into the lot behind the clubhouse. Only a few other cars were parked there.

Orville, Agatha, and Mr. Wright found Mrs. Wright in the banquet hall part of the center clubhouse. *The giganto, tremendo, could-hold-half-of-Bottomless-Lake banquet hall part of the clubhouse*, Agatha thought, taking in the room's immensity.

"Mr. Beck? Trey?" Mrs. Wright was calling in a strange, giggly, high-pitched voice.

"Look. There's a Trey Beck in the center of the room," Orville pointed out.

"Yeah, but that Trey Beck is double life size and made of ice," Agatha said. "Come on. Let's check it out!"

Agatha and Orville approached the ice sculpture of Trey Beck. Agatha had never seen an ice sculpture up close before. The purple and blue flowers of the center-pieces on the tables were reflected in the statue's wet, shiny surface. It made Agatha want to lick it. But she restrained herself, knowing that tongue-glued-to-ice-sculpture was not an attractive look for anyone.

"Trey?" Mrs. Wright called again.

"I think he's in the kids' area," a woman answered from the back of the ballroom.

"That's June, the florist," Orville filled in. "My mother has talked to her an average of 2.5 times per week over the last six months . . . with a sharp increase to 3.2 times within the last two weeks."

June flicked a light switch and tiny white lightbulbs began to shine in the flower arrangements. Agatha gasped. The whole place looked magical!

"Very nice, June. Thank you," Mrs. Wright said. She reached over and plucked a blossom from one of the vases, frowning. "Although these forget-me-nots have a bit of a yellow tinge to them. They'll all need to be replaced."

Agatha's mouth dropped open, but not as far open as the florist's. Orville's mother didn't seem to notice. She just clack-clacked out of the hall and up a wide flight of stairs. Agatha, Orville, and Mr. Wright followed along behind her like ducklings.

At the top of the stairs, Mrs. Wright pushed through the door. Agatha stepped into the room and couldn't believe her eyes.

This . . . was the *kids' area*?

A motorized rock-climbing wall dominated the left side of the football-field-size space. Three Dance Dance Revolution games stood side by side on the right, with an entrance to a 3-D movie theater next to them. A slew of arcade games and virtual reality pods ran up and down the center of the place.

"You've got dog-with-dinosaur-bone face," Orville observed. That was the expression Agatha had come up with to describe the combo of a big goofy grin, wide eyes, and an optional trickle of drool down the chin.

"Do you blame me?" Agatha asked.

She did a quick chin check. Whew. No drool. But she was without a doubt drooling on the inside. There were a million cool games in here!

Agatha turned and noticed a hang glider simulator on the left. Amazing! Orville dreamed of soaring through the sky. He'd love that one. Ooh, and there was a Ferrari-driving simulator too. Agatha's foot itched to get in and floor it.

The door to the 3-D theater opened, and the man of the hour, Trey Beck, stepped out. "*The Cadburys* should be filmed in 3-D," he called as he walked toward them. "Don't you think?"

Agatha had always believed that no actual humans looked as good as the people on TV. But Trey looked exactly the way he did on *The Cadburys*. His curly blond hair was just as shiny, his lime-Life-Saver-green eyes just as bright, his muscles as muscle-y. He *was* a little shorter than he looked on the tube. But that just made him closer to Agatha size. Who needed a six-foot giant when you weren't even five feet tall?

"It's already possible to watch the show in 3-D," Orville informed Trey. "There is an adapter available that creates left-eye and right-eye images on your TV and displays them in an alternating format. You have to wear 3-D glasses. They receive a signal that causes the lenses to open and close along with the images on the screen so each eye receives only the correct images, and that produces stereographic three dimensions."

Agatha winced. This was the moment when strangers usually stared at Orville as if he were an insane six-headed super-nerd. They just didn't know what to make of Orville, especially when he was being trying to be helpful like this. But much to Agatha's surprise, Trey didn't stare. Instead, he pulled out a mini–cassette recorder and spoke into it. "Rick, I'm gonna need one of those 3-D TV adapter things—stat! I want it hooked up and ready to go within one hour after you receive this message." He slid the recorder back into his pocket. "I told my assistant he could have the night off to do some shopping for me, so I have to tape instructions for him while he's away."

Agatha and Orville nodded. For one brief, shining moment, Agatha wondered what it would be like to have an assistant of her own.

Mmmm. Her assistant's main task would be to bring her fabulous lipsticks aplenty. . . .

Trey stepped up to Mrs. Wright and gave her a hug. "Elaine. Good to see you. Were you able to tell the photographers that I don't like to be shot from the left?"

"It's all taken care of," Mrs. Wright said when Trey released her. "But I don't think you should worry. I don't believe anyone could possibly take a bad picture of you."

Agatha shot a glance at Mr. Wright to see if it both-ered him that his wife was full-on flirting with her favorite soap star. It didn't seem to. It *did* seem to bother him when Trey gave him a long back-thumping embrace of his own.

Then Trey turned to Orville. He extended his arms. . . .

"Don't!" Agatha and the Wrights cried.

A confused expression flitted over Trey's chiseled features.

"It's his condition. He doesn't like to be touched," Mrs. Wright explained.

"I'm fine with it!" Agatha jumped in. "Hug me!"

Trey grinned and swung her off her feet in a hug that she thought might be even better than hang gliding. When Trey returned her to the ground, her head felt fizzy. She struggled to keep from smiling like a total buffoon. She—Agatha Wong—had been embraced by a super-cute TV celebrity!

"Let me take you downstairs and show you the seat-ing plan," Mrs. Wright told Trey. "I've put you between Mrs. Doheny, one of Placid's most prominent citizens, and myself."

"I hope you'll be serving up the armadillo meat I asked for," Trey said. "I can't visit Arizona without eat-ing an armadillo. I always try the local meat wherever I go. And—bonus—a three-ounce serving of armadillo has only 150 calories. That's less than possum and squirrel."

He wants to eat an armadillo? Agatha wondered. *But they're so tiny and . . . scaly. Ew.*

"It was a bit difficult. Armadillos *are* common in Arizona, but not as food," Mrs. Wright said. "Luckily we were able to find some. We're serving up a special armadillo steak just for you, with a jalapeño marinade."

"Jalapeños?" Trey shook his head. "No, no. I don't do jalapeños. Didn't you read my list of forbidden foods? Those peppers make my eyes water, and when my eyes water, they get bloodshot. And soap stars can't have that!"

"It's just for flavoring. I'm sure it won't be strong enough to make you tear up," Mrs. Wright said quickly. "And it wasn't on the list. I studied it very carefully."

"Huh. Maybe Rick didn't give you the latest one. I'm always updating," Trey replied. He pulled out his mini-recorder again. "Rick, make sure you're giving out the most recent forbidden-food list. There has been an incident at the party tonight." He clicked off the recorder. "I can't risk the sauce, Elaine. I'm shooting tomorrow. You understand."

Mrs. Wright nibbled at her lower lip, eating off some of her lipstick. "Of course. I'll just run into the kitchen and consult with the chef. Now come with me, and I'll get you a glass of the *colpisca l'acqua leggermente* you requested."

"Great!" Trey smiled, following Orville's mom from

the room. "It's the water preferred by emperors everywhere. It says so on the bottle."

Agatha waited until Trey and Orville's parents were
out of earshot—then she let loose. "Armadillo?
Jalapeño? *Acqua de who-ja-ma-whatsis?* That guy is the
walking, talking definition of high maintenance."

"And that water he was talking about," Orville put
in. "It's not possible that it is preferred by emperors.
There are no emperors in modern times."

Agatha chuckled. "I guess we should be glad he
didn't ask your mother to serve him a slab of Trixie on a
stick, since sea monster is our other local meat."

Orville frowned. "That also would be impossible
since—"

"I know, I know," Agatha interrupted. "Since Trixie,
the Bottomless Lake monster, couldn't possibly exist."

This bit about Trixie was one of Orville's favorite
refrains. It drove Agatha's nana—the owner of a successful sea monster souvenir shop—crazy, but it just
made Agatha smile. Her best friend was totally one of
a kind.

"So what do we do first?" Agatha nodded toward a
kayak resting on what looked like a giant high-tech
rocking chair. "You want to try the boat simulator? We
can do that together."

"Can I come too?" a voice called.

Agatha turned and found Tim Gore smiling at her.

Tim and his sister, Tina, had gone to elementary school in Bottomless Lake with Agatha and Orville, but his family had moved to Placid last year.

"What are you doing here so early?" Agatha asked. "Is it time for the party to start already?"

Tim shook his head. "My mother always confuses fashionably late with fashionably early. We're twenty minutes early everywhere we go. So . . . can we kayak?"

Agatha studied Tim.

Had his time in Placid, aka Snootsville, changed him?

He hadn't learned that his hair should be cut the instant it reached his ears and started to curl up at the ends like a baby's. So he wasn't ultra-fashionable. And he was acting fully friendly, with no you-must-be-blemished-because-you're-from-Bottomless-Lake pose.

Agatha squinted at Tim and decided he hadn't turned into a typical Placid snob . . . yet.

"Come on," she told him. "The more the et cetera."

"So what's up?" Tim asked as he, Agatha, and Orville headed to the kayak. "I heard you guys solved another case after the one at our school. Are you working on a new mystery right now? Got anything on the burner?"

"It's extremely unsafe to leave a stove on unattended," Orville answered, taking Tim's words literally.

"What Orville means is no," Agatha translated. "We

are currently in a mystery-free zone. We have nothing on our minds but enjoying ourselves. So let's go!"

Agatha and Orville enjoyed themselves in the mystery-free zone for four more hours. The kids' area filled with people from Placid. But they were all so busy playing, dancing, and rock climbing that nobody even bothered to ask a snotty question about Agatha, Orville, and Bottomless Lake. It was the best night ever!

Then came the scream from downstairs.

Agatha didn't even think. She just jumped off her DDR machine and bolted down the staircase to the banquet hall. Everyone in the place was staring at a red-headed woman in a long, sleek silver gown.

Agatha's eyes darted over the woman. No blood. No broken bones. Not even a nasty, dripping soon-to-be stain. Nothing that should have caused that unholy shriek.

"What's wrong? What happened?" Agatha blurted as Orville stumbled to a halt next to her.

"I'll tell you what's wrong. Someone stole my bracelet!" the woman shot back.

"Are you sure you wore it tonight, Chloe?" Orville's mom asked, rushing toward the woman.

"Maybe *you* own the kind of jewelry you can forget about," Chloe answered. "But I don't. I'm certain I put it on tonight. It was Barry Kronen, from his Victorian Lace collection."

"Ouch. That's seventeen grand down the drain," someone behind Agatha muttered.

Agatha's stomach flip-flopped. Seventeen grand? As in smackers? Samoleans? Seventeen thousand *dollars*? That was a lot of money for one bracelet.

"Perhaps it simply fell off," Mrs. Wright suggested. "Everyone, would you please look around your feet and by your table for—"

She was interrupted by women from every corner of the room.

"My Kazto flower ring! It's gone too!"

"My Le Vian pin is missing!"

"My Erica Courtney clover pendant! It was right here on my lapel!"

Mrs. Wright clapped. "Everyone! Please. Calm down."

But no one listened. The raised voices echoed off the high domed ceiling. They grew louder and louder.

Then a fifty-something woman in a strapless black dress stepped up to Mrs. Wright.

"Your attention," the black-haired woman commanded. The room went silent.

"Thank you, Mrs. Doheny," Mrs. Wright said.

Ooh! It's the big Doheny, Agatha realized. *Chairwoman of this, president of that. No wonder all these hysterical Placidians listen to her.*

"Here's what I think we should do," Mrs. Wright continued. "I'll make a list of—"

"I think it's time to say good night," Mrs. Doheny cut her off. "Let's all thank Mr. Trey Beck for his presence here tonight and especially for his patience in posing for all those pictures with us." She led a round of applause. "And our hostess for the evening, Mrs. Elaine Wright."

Agatha applauded as hard as she could for Orville's mom. She was pretty much the only one not related to Mrs. Wright who did.

"We'll hold a meeting to discuss the thefts. I'll activate the phone tree," Mrs. Doheny called. "Now, it's time to say goodbye. Night-night, everyone." She started toward the huge doors leading out of the hall, then paused at the table behind Orville and Agatha to pick up her evening bag. Chloe, the redheaded woman, followed her.

"I'm so glad you're going to take charge of the situation," Chloe said, her voice still shaking.

"Well, I certainly couldn't let Elaine Wright handle it," Mrs. Doheny replied, raising her voice so that everyone around her could hear. "Poor thing. I'm sure it was too much temptation. All these pretty things that she knows she'll never have for herself. She must have simply snapped."

Agatha turned to Orville. His face was blank. But deep in his eyes she saw the same outrage she was feeling burbling inside.

"So you think *she's* the thief?" Chloe cried, scandalized.

"Who else?" Mrs. Doheny answered. With that, she left the ballroom in a swirl of black taffeta.

"My mother didn't steal anything," Orville told Agatha.

"You don't even have to say that," Agatha answered, clenching her fists. "I know she didn't."

She scanned the ballroom, her eyes moving over all the beautiful people in their beautiful clothes. Most of them were whispering, nudging one another, and shooting glances at Mrs. Wright. "But someone who was here tonight did steal that jewelry, Orville. And we are going to find out who!"

Chapter 2

"Mrs. Doheny thinks I'm a thief."

Orville's mother was sitting several tables away. Orville could hear those same six words each time his mother said them—approximately every fifteen seconds since the party ended.

Orville had noted that the words had an effect on his pulse. Each time they came out of his mother's mouth, his pulse picked up between ten to twelve beats per minute. He considered the possibility that he might be nervous, but he didn't have any of the other physical sensations that came with nervousness. The spaces between his fingers were dry. His throat was moist. His legs felt solid, not wobbly—

"I know you're angry," Agatha said, pulling him out of his thoughts. "Scream if you want to. Or punch something. Punch that laundry bag." She nodded toward the canvas bag loaded with the tablecloths and napkins she and Orville were gathering up.

"Why?" Orville asked.

"It helps. When I'm mad, I like to punch. And now that we're in middle school and it's not socially acceptable to punch *people*, even when they extremely deserve it, I've moved on to punching inanimate objects. The laundry bag is good. Nothing in there that will damage those little bones in your hand."

"Mrs. Doheny thinks I'm a thief," Mrs. Wright wailed.

Out of the corner of his eye, Orville saw his mother lower her head into her hands. His pulse picked up again.

Anger? Was that why his pulse kept accelerating?

"If some evil, black-haired salon dweller called my mom a thief, I'd be nuclear," Agatha said. She moved to the next table and snatched up all the napkins. "Seven," she told Orville. He added the number to his running total. His mother needed to know that every napkin and tablecloth was accounted for.

"So get whamming on that bag," Agatha instructed. "Then we'll come up with a list of possible suspects."

"I don't think punching the laundry will help," Orville said.

"Yeah. You're probably right. It makes you a little tired, though. And if you do it enough, it gives you excellent biceps." Agatha flexed so Orville could see her arm muscles.

They were indeed admirable.

She moved on to another table, closer to Orville's parents.

"Mrs. Doheny thinks I'm a thief," Orville's mother said. Her words were muffled by her hands, but Orville still heard them. His pulse responded.

"So if we're skipping the punching part of our agenda, we're on to suspects," Agatha said. "All two hundred of them—that's how many guests were at this shindig, right?"

"Two hundred and eleven," Orville corrected. "And sixteen waiters, one florist, one head caterer, a chef and four assistants, one photographer, and two dish-washers."

"So that's . . ." Agatha's fingers twitched as she silently counted.

"Two hundred and thirty-seven," Orville told her.

Agatha let out a long, soft whistle. "Two hundred and thirty-seven suspects. That's one heck of a heap. But some of them must be more suspicious than others. How do you think we should start?" She pulled off the tablecloth and jammed it into the laundry bag along with the napkins.

"We should look for patterns," Orville answered. Finding patterns was an excellent way to narrow down a suspect list. He'd been thinking about it ever since he and Agatha had solved their first mystery at the begin-ning of the school year. As far as he could tell, people who committed crimes existed outside the patterns of normal behavior. He hadn't mentioned this theory to Agatha yet. It lacked the proper proof. But tonight could be the perfect test.

He hurried over to his mother and asked her for the

map of the ballroom that showed how all the guests were seated, then returned to Agatha. With his favorite yellow highlighter, he colored the names of the seventeen women who'd had jewelry stolen.

Agatha squinted at the paper. "I'm not seeing any pattern. Although if this were a connect the dots, it would make a kind of a rabbit. If you left out a few dots. And squinted."

Orville let his eyes roam over the yellow marks. He noted a grouping that formed the structural formula for acetic acid, with Mrs. Doheny as one of the two carbon atoms. But there was no rabbit. At least, none that he could see.

"What are you thinking? Tell me," Agatha urged, her words coming out twenty-one percent faster than her norm, which was already fourteen percent faster than the average person's.

"I just noticed the formula for acetic acid." Orville ran his finger over what would be the bonds between the atoms.

"I don't think that or the rabbit will help us. Unless we have one very twisted jewel thief on our hands. Someone who knows that the detectives tracking him down have a combined knowledge of both the animal kingdom and chemistry. Someone who is almost begging to be caught by leaving clues that—" Agatha pressed her hands over her mouth. "Why don't you stop me when I start to projectile-spew?"

Orville tried to translate from Agatha to English. She was not projectile-spewing anything. Had she been about to vomit? Or was there another meaning? Sometimes it was hard to tell with Agatha. She liked to say she used the English language creatively. Orville thought she just used it incorrectly.

"So do we agree that the seating arrangement of the victims gives us nothing?" Agatha asked. "I mean, we have one table with seven victims, some tables with none, one table with one, one over there with three. . . ."

"I agree," Orville said. "There doesn't seem to be a geographic pattern to the thefts."

"Wait!" Agatha yelped. "Rewind, okay? Back to the part where you were telling me about the numbers of servant types. You said photographer, didn't you? Please tell me you said photographer."

"Yes. I said photographer," Orville answered. "There was one photographer covering the event."

Agatha whirled around. "Mrs. Wright!" she called. "Did the photographer go home?"

Orville's mother lifted her head off the table and stared at Agatha for 6.2 seconds. She didn't say anything. Which was extremely unusual.

Orville's father spoke up instead. "She hasn't collected her check, so I'm sure she hasn't left. Some of the workers are eating in the kitch—"

Agatha didn't wait for him to finish. She raced toward the kitchen. Orville followed her.

"Photographer. We need the photographer!" Agatha yelled as soon as they stepped inside.

A woman stood up from the table. She had short hair of a reddish orange color. *The same reddish orange as the moon during the last lunar eclipse*, Orville noted. She held a forkful of salad in her hand, a glob of blue cheese dressing about to plop onto the floor.

"You need a photographer? You got one," the woman said. "The name's Marti. Did someone miss out on their chance for a photo with Trey Beck?"

"Nuh-uh," Agatha answered. "Well, actually I did, and it would have been kinda chillsome to have one, but listen, did you take digital pictures or the on-film kind?"

"I'm digital all the way, baby," Marti bragged.

"Great. Can we look at what you shot?" Agatha asked. She pointed to Orville. "His mom organized the whole thing."

Marti ate the bite of salad, then put down her fork. "Press here to advance," she told Agatha as she handed her the camera. "Here's the other memory card."

"You look," Agatha told Orville, passing the camera. "You're detail guy. See if there are any details worth noticing."

Orville gazed at the camera's digital screen, slowly studying each picture. When he was done, Agatha changed the memory card and he continued going through the tiny images. When he was done with that card too, he gave the camera back to Marti. He remembered to say thank you—and to smile, just the way his social skills teacher, Miss Eloise, had instructed in her lesson "gratitude needs attitude."

Agatha led the way back to the table where they'd left off their laundry collection. "So what did you see in the photos? Anything juicy?"

"Juicy?" Orville repeated.

"Wrong word. Did you see anything, um, important?" Agatha asked. "Anything that could be a clue? Tell me everything you noticed. "

Orville took a deep breath before beginning. "There were three hundred and one pictures. All but seven had people in them. Approximately twelve percent of the men were wearing bow ties. In the photos where people were eating, it appeared that eight percent were left-handed, which is approximately three percent less than the national average."

"Albert L. Placid probably discourages left-handedness. It's too unusual for his perfect little town." Agatha snorted. "What about the jewelry? Was it on the women in the pictures?"

"There were pictures of all the thief's victims with

their jewelry, with Trey Beck, and without their jewelry," Orville answered.

"And I guess you saw nothing that would make our job easier. Like a hand with a really distinctive tattoo snatching a bracelet?"

"No," Orville told her.

Agatha sighed. "A girl can dream. So go on. What else?"

"Approximately three percent of the people ate the armadillo. Trey Beck was always photographed straight on or from the right. He appeared in one hundred and eight of the pictures."

"Zowie. I guess everyone in the place wanted their picture taken with Ryan Cadbur—" Agatha paused. Her pupils widened slightly and her breath came a little faster. "Oh, wait a second. Watch out, Orville. I'm having a brain tsunami. Did you say that all the women who had jewelry stolen got their picture taken with Trey?" She moved to the table next to Orville's parents and started to gather up the napkins.

"Yes," Orville answered. "Every woman at the party had her picture taken with him. There were only three men who didn't. One of them was my dad."

Agatha waved the napkins over her head and performed what she referred to as her happy dance. "Oh, yeah," she called. "I'm a genius."

"Most people say genius starts at one hundred and

forty or one hundred and forty-five on the Wechsler Intelligence Scale," Orville informed her.

"Well, one hundred and forty-five must be my number—because I have closed the case!" Agatha cried. "Trey Beck is our jewel thief!"

"No! That's not possible."

Orville whirled around. Those were the first words other than "Mrs. Doheny thinks I'm a thief" that his mother had uttered in the last forty-seven minutes and twenty seconds.

"I know what you're thinking," Agatha answered. "Why would a soap star steal anything? He should be able to buy whatever he wants. But the thief would have needed an excuse put his hands on all his victims. The picture is the perfect way!"

"Trey *was* touching all the women he was photographed with—and eighty-four percent of the men," Orville confirmed. "And it was clear from the order of the photos that the victims all had their jewelry before posing with Trey."

"Exactly!" Agatha continued. "Before their pictures with Trey, the women had jewelry. After the pictures, just skin. Of the very well-moisturized and massaged variety, I'm sure—but either way, Trey Beck is our number-one suspect."

"No. Trey Beck is a beautiful, heroic man," Orville's mother insisted. "He would never steal from anyone.

He didn't have to come to our charity event at all. He did it out of the goodness of his heart because he cares about people. I don't want to hear one more negative word about him."

Orville noticed that his mother's hands were tightened into fists and her whole body was vibrating. He wondered if an accelerometer would indicate that she had changed frequencies.

Agatha opened her mouth, shut it, opened it again, shut it. Finally she asked, "Did you see anyone *else* acting suspicious at the party, Mrs. Wright?"

"I didn't see anything unusual," Orville's mother answered. "But I'll bet you Mrs. Doheny is the thief. She would do anything to make me look bad—even ruin the fund-raiser for the Cheerful Community committee."

"Wait—didn't you say that she's co-chair of the committee?" Agatha asked.

"Yes," Orville answered for his mother.

"*That's* how much she despises me," Mrs. Wright went on. "She didn't want me to organize the party. She was on vacation when the other chairperson gave her approval. Mrs. Doheny doesn't think I'm Placid material. She doesn't think anyone from Bottomless Lake is good enough for this town."

"Wow. What a complete broomstick rider," Agatha whispered.

Orville's mom nodded. "She stole the jewels so tonight would be a disaster and everyone would think that she was right—that I'm no good."

"Don't worry, Mom. We're going to prove that you didn't steal the jewels," Orville said.

"We are," Agatha agreed. She reached out and put her arm around Orville's mother's shoulders.

Orville felt a little twist in his stomach. He wished he could be like Agatha. Not in every way. But in the way of being able to connect with people. To hug them. To let them know how you felt.

"And you know what?" Agatha continued. "We're going to start by investigating Mrs. Thinks-she's-so-much-better-than-you-and-is-so-so-wrong Doheny. If she's the thief, we'll take her down!"

Orville frowned. "Down where?"

"Is this woman's butt made of gold or what?" Chris Pearson demanded.

"There is almost no chance of her butt being made of gold," Orville said. "It would not be biologically viable."

"Then what's with the security?" Chris asked. He blew a big gum bubble. "You said it was high-tech. But this is off the grid."

"That's why we called you," Agatha said, peeking at the home of Mrs. My-butt-thinks-it's-made-of-gold-and-is-so-so-wrong Doheny. "Orville said you were some kind of mad techno genius. We have no problem doing surveillance in our town. But in Bottomless Lake the biggest snooping obstacle is curtains. This," she said, pointing to the ten small cameras keeping watch on the Doheny estate, "is a whole different ball game."

Chris whistled and shoved his long brown hair out of his eyes. "You can say that again. This system has photo-infrared sensors that can recognize familiar people and keep out strangers. It can even recognize your dog. If you have a dog."

"We're standing out of range," Orville filled in. "So it hasn't detected us."

"The system also has sound sensors," Chris continued. "It can tell the difference between a window smashing and a plate breaking, so it doesn't call in an alarm just because you're clumsy like Orville."

"Hey!" Agatha protested.

"What?" Orville and Chris asked together.

"You just insulted my friend," Agatha told Chris.

"I did?" Chris asked.

"He did?" Orville echoed.

Agatha drew in a breath and reminded herself that Orville knew Chris through social skills class. Which meant that Chris, like Orville, had some social skills issues of his own.

"You called Orville clumsy," she said gently. "That wasn't very nice."

"He *is* clumsy," Chris answered.

"I am," Orville agreed. "Chris was stating a fact."

"I know," Agatha said. "But it's still not a nice thing to say."

"See it doesn't mean say it," Orville helpfully reminded Chris, clearly quoting their social skills teacher.

"Okay," Chris replied. "So who am I supposed to apologize to? You?" He jabbed his finger at Agatha. "Because you're the one who has her underpants in a twist? Or him—because I said it about him? Even though he doesn't care."

"Uh, good question," Agatha said. Unfortunately, she didn't know the answer. How did Miss Eloise figure out all this stuff? "You know what? Forget about all that. Let's just focus. Do you think you can get us close enough to the house to peek inside?"

"It would help if we had one of Mrs. Doheny's fingers," Chris answered.

"Excuse me?" Agatha said.

"Mrs. Doheny's finger. For her fingerprint," Chris explained. "But since that's probably not possible . . ."

"Duh," Agatha confirmed.

". . . I have another plan. My cousin is a total bad egg. He's always sneaking out at night. His parents got a system sort of like this so that he couldn't lie about what time he got home." Chris chuckled. "They should have cut off his allowance instead. Because he paid me the big bucks to come up with a way to disable it."

Chris pulled an electronic . . . *thingie* out of his backpack. It looked like a mutant phone/text messenger/Game Boy.

"First," Chris said, "we gotta set up a little cross talk."

"What's that?" Agatha asked.

"You're probably not smart enough to understand, and it would take too long to explain," Chris blurted.

Agatha took a deep breath and told herself to remain calm. Punching was not mature—and Chris couldn't help his bluntness. "Try me," she said through gritted teeth.

"Let's just say that this"—Chris shook the handheld thingie—"is going to talk really loud over the signal being sent by the security cameras. This will confuse the cameras and shut them down." Chris punched a few buttons, then gave a satisfied smile. A smug smile. Like he thought *his* butt was made of gold.

Agatha wanted more than ever to tell him to go home and get in some practice on his apologies. But she and Orville needed him to get close to Mrs. Doheny.

"Is that it?" Agatha asked. "Is it done?"

"Of course not," Chris shot back sarcastically, chomping harder on his gum. "You can't override a twenty-thousand-dollar security system with a modified Game Boy." He shook his head, then took a laptop out of his backpack. "Wireless. A little bonus from my cousin." He powered up, then let his fingers fly over the keyboard.

"Adjusting the modulation of the local loop transmission won't be enough to disable the video," Orville explained.

"Uh-huh," Agatha grunted, trying—and failing—to follow along. She reminded herself that she was plenty brainy—she just had different brain storage priorities.

"I'm also tweaking the passband, doing some compression with the wavelets, and fiddling the delay," Chris added. He entered a few more codes.

"Okay," he said, closing the laptop. "Last step, cornstarch."

"Cornstarch?" Orville asked.

Immediately Agatha felt better. If *Orville* didn't understand something, she couldn't possibly feel stupid.

"Yep." Chris pulled a box of cornstarch out of his backpack. "The cameras are taken care of, so now we can get close enough to use it."

He trotted toward the gate in front of the Doheny house. Agatha and Orville exchanged glances, then trotted after him. Chris scooped out a handful of cornstarch and leaned down until his mouth was even with the gate keypad. He blew the powdery stuff off his palm. "It sticks to the keys that are used most frequently because of the oil on people's fingers," he explained.

Agatha checked out the pad. Four keys were definitely a lot more cornstarched than the others. Those keys had to be the ones in the combination.

"Yes!" Chris cheered. "A round of applause, please. Come on, people, give it up!" He waited.

And waited.

Finally Agatha gave it up, and a moment later Orville started to clap too.

"Thank you. Thank you," Chris said, bowing deeply.

"So, how many numbers are in the combination?" Orville asked.

"The combination for this particular model is five numbers," Chris stated.

"But only four keys are cornstarched. That means one number repeats. It also means you have sixteen possible combinations," Orville observed.

"Yep," Chris said, dusting the cornstarch off his hands. "Of course, this puppy's not going to let me make sixteen guesses. It'll give me three."

"I'm not loving those odds," Agatha commented.

Chris blew another bubble. "Well, most people are dumb, so that helps. They don't use truly random number combos. People like patterns. These four numbers can make a diamond pattern. I'm gonna try that, starting with the number three, 'cause it's on the left.

People also like the left-to-right thing. And I'm going to hit three again when I work my way around to it." He punched in the numbers—

Beep, beep, beep. CLICK!

Agatha heard the sweet, sweet sound of the gate opening. "Nice," she said, truly impressed.

"Yup. Let's move," Chris said. He took a step forward.

"Whoa. Whoa, whoa, whoa." Agatha blocked his path. "Where do you think you're going? We can't *all* sneak in there. Three people are easier to catch than two."

"One of you go home, then," Chris answered. "I opened the shell—now I want a peek at the nut."

He scooted around Agatha and walked right onto Mrs. Doheny's billion-acre front lawn.

"All right." Agatha darted after him. "You can come, but let me give you the low-tech lowdown. Those glass things at the front of the house? Those are windows. People can see through them. And unless you modulated their eyeballs, you are completely visible to any human who happens to glance outside."

Orville nodded. "Like Agatha says, you've got to tree-to-tree it."

Fortunately, the Doheny lawn had a lot of trees. Agatha, Orville, and Chris scurried from one tree to the next, staying out in the open as little as possible. When they reached the tree closest to Mrs. Doheny's house, Orville peeked around the gigantic trunk.

"What do you see?" Agatha asked.

"Mrs. Doheny—dining with a guest," Orville reported.

"Who?" Agatha asked.

"Trey Beck," Orville answered.

Agatha gasped. "Oh my gosh. Our number-one suspect!"

"Trey Beck?" Chris repeated. "Who's that?"

Oh, Agatha wanted to say, *guess you don't know everything, do you, Mr. Smartypants?* But even to her, that sounded like a third grader in the middle of a snit fit.

"He's the star of a soap opera," she finally answered in her most mature voice.

"The window is open," Orville pointed out.

"Really? I'm shocked and stunned," Agatha said. "Who knew people in Placid allowed themselves to breathe un-conditioned air?"

Agatha peeked around the tree trunk. She scanned the area in front of the window. "I think there's room for all of us behind the azaleas. But we're going to have to crawl to get into position. Everybody ready? Come on!"

She dropped to her belly and scrambled over the grass. She wedged herself between the front wall of the house and the flowery bushes. Chris squeezed in next to her. Orville scrunched himself into a ball so he could maintain his required one foot of space on all sides. He hated to be touched.

"Hey, did you hear they're planning another *Matrix* movie?" Chris asked. "All me. I started a letter-writing campaign."

"No talking!" Agatha whispered. She pointed up. "Open window."

She twisted around and straightened up just enough for her eyes to clear the bottom of the windowsill.

She realized that if she listened carefully, she could make out Trey and Mrs. Doheny's conversation.

Blah, blah, blah. Trey couldn't eat anything with kale. Blah, blah, blah. Mrs. Doheny just loved *The Cadburys*, and if Trey's character was killed off, Mrs. Doheny would just die herself. Blah, blah, blah. Mrs. Doheny was so sorry that the party was ruined by Mrs. Wright and her sticky fingers.

"Hey!" Agatha burst out. She couldn't help herself. The word just exploded out of her when she heard Mrs. Doheny blaming Mrs. Wright!

Agatha stood stock-still. She didn't even blink as she waited for a reaction from Trey or Mrs. Doheny. After a second or two, they just kept on blabbing.

Agatha closed her eyes and let out a sigh of relief. When she opened them again, she almost gave another "Hey!"

Trey Beck was sliding a diamond-studded watch off Mrs. Doheny's wrist!

"Man, stalkers are getting younger every day," a voice called from behind her. Agatha jerked her head around. A twenty-something guy with spiky hair stood on the other side of the azaleas.

Oh, no. Busted!

Chapter 3

"Come out of there and I'll give you each an autographed photo of Trey," the guy on the lawn said. "I'll also give you a five-minute head start before I call the cops."

Agatha's brain went into overdrive. This guy thought she was snooping because she was one of Trey's fans?

Excellent! She silently thanked the Big Kahuna in the sky that Spiky Hair had given them the perfect excuse.

"Great! A picture of Trey. Wow!" Agatha gushed. "I'm his biggest, biggest fan." She pushed herself to her feet and wriggled out of her hiding place.

Spiky Hair handed her a photo. Agatha kissed it—just to help her performance reach Oscar level. "Thanks so much for not sending us downtown."

"I've seen much worse than three kids staring at Trey from a safe distance," the guy said. "By the way, just so you know who to be grateful to, I'm Rick Muirragui, Trey's hardworking assistant and stalker shooer."

"Well, thanks again, Rick," Agatha said. "We've got to go. I want to get this laminated!" Agatha stroked her

Trey picture, compensating for Chris and Orville's extreme lack of faux interest in their photos. " 'Bye!"

She led the charge to the gate, skidding to a stop the moment her feet hit the pavement. The boys followed more slowly.

"Do you know who this is a picture of?" Agatha demanded.

"Duh, you just told me ten minutes ago. Troy Beck," Chris answered.

"*Trey* Beck," Agatha corrected.

"Tray? That's not a name," Chris scoffed. "That's something you carry your food on."

He was ruining her moment. Agatha decided to ignore him.

"Orville," she said. "Right here in my hand is a photo of Trey Beck, who I just saw nab Mrs. Doheny's watch. This is a picture of our jewelry thief! All we need now is to prove it!"

Orville stood in front of his open locker. His pulse rate was thirty-three percent higher than usual. His throat was moist. The spaces between his fingers were dry. The back of his neck felt seven percent hotter than usual.

He remembered standing in the banquet hall listening to his mother say, "Mrs. Doheny thinks I'm a thief." The back of his neck had felt approximately seven percent hotter at that time too.

"Say that again," he told Stu Frysley.

Stu grinned. "I said, how does it feel to have a thief for a mom? Does she give you a cut of the cash so you won't turn her in?"

Orville checked his physical symptoms again. Yes, they definitely matched the ones he'd experienced last night. Interesting . . .

"Shut up, Stubert!" Agatha yelled from next to Orville. "How dare you accuse an innocent woman! We're going to sue you for libel, for assassination of character, for—for being a big idiot!"

Orville looked at Agatha. Her face was sixty-one percent redder than usual and her respiration was fast. He knew those symptoms—they meant she was angry.

Perhaps his collection of strange physical symptoms meant that he was angry as well. Agatha had told him he was feeling mad when he'd experienced them at the party. Perhaps she was right.

"You are making me angry," he told Stu.

"What?" Agatha cried, her eyes going wide. "Are you kidding me? Go, Orville! Get down with your bad self. You're mad and you should be. Stu is an ignorant pig. No, that's an insult to Esther and Jeremy. Stu is an ignorant . . . Stu."

Stu stuck his tongue out. "Everyone knows it's true, *Ag*normal. Orville's mom stole jewelry from a bunch of froufrou ladies at some Placid party. My mom says his mom made every single person in Bottomless Lake look bad."

"Well, *you* do that just by being alive," Agatha shot back.

"My mother didn't steal anything," Orville said, his pulse and the temperature of the back of his neck rising even higher. He felt himself begin to blink rapidly. His body began to shake. He made a mental note to add accelerated blinking and tremors to his list of anger symptoms.

"What's he doing?" Stu asked, taking a step back. "He looks like he's going to blow."

"You've been tormenting Orville since birth, and he's never once gotten mad," Agatha replied. "That's a lot of built-up rage, Stu. Rage that could level everything within three blocks. If I were you, I'd—"

Stu didn't wait to hear Agatha's advice. He turned and ran off down the crowded hallway.

Agatha laughed. "Well, that was quite enjoyable." She turned to Orville. "Hey. Are you all right?"

"Yes," Orville said, staring after Stu, who almost fell as he took the corner at the end of the hall.

"Scaredy-cat Stu. I could watch that all day," Agatha said. "Unfortunately, we've got work to do. Look what I found on the bulletin board outside the caf."

She handed Orville a flyer.

" 'Items from the bulletin board may only be removed

by faculty or administration,'" Orville said, quoting from the John Q. Adams Middle School handbook.

"Don't worry. I'll put it back," Agatha told him. "But read it first."

Orville read the flyer. The director of *The Cadburys* was holding an acting contest for kids age eight to fourteen at the Placid mall. The winner would get a speaking role on an episode of the show.

"You want to be an actress?" Orville asked. Agatha had never mentioned that before. In second grade, she'd wanted to be a spy or a hula girl. In third grade, she'd wanted to be a helicopter pilot or a hairdresser. In fourth, she'd again wanted to be a spy, a spy with fabulous hair who could fly a helicopter and sometimes went undercover as a hula girl. In fifth, a vet specializing in exotic animals. In sixth, a chef. In seventh . . .

Orville scanned his memory files. In seventh, she hadn't yet mentioned a career goal.

"No, silly. I don't want to be an actress," Agatha said. "Though I bet being in the business has some tasty perks. And I do have a flair for the dramatic. But that's not the point. One of us has to win this contest, because we need to get close to Trey Beck so that we can hunt for and gather proof that he's the thief. We can't get much closer than being on the show with him, so—" She took a deep breath. Frequently Agatha exhausted her air supply before reaching the end of a sentence.

"*One of us* has to win?" Orville asked. "You want *me* to be in the acting contest?"

Moisture flooded the crevices between his fingers. He knew it was biologically impossible, but it felt like the wetness had traveled from his throat, which was now very dry.

Orville decided he wasn't mad anymore, even though his pulse was accelerating again. Now he was anxious—severely anxious.

"If we both enter the contest, we have better odds of winning it," Agatha answered. "And sometimes in showbiz it's all about how you look, not about actual acting talent. Maybe the director is looking for a sandy-haired almost-thirteen-year-old with good posture. If so, he's not going to pick me. He's going to pick you, my friend."

Orville immediately began trying to calculate the odds that the director was looking for a sandy-haired almost-thirteen-year-old. He was still working on the calculations when he and Agatha entered the cool—he estimated its temperature to be sixty-nine degrees—air of the Placid mall after school.

"This place smells like nothing," Agatha said. "The Bottomless Lake mall smells like popcorn and perfume and hair-dyeing chemicals. It smells *alive*. This place smells . . . empty."

Orville sniffed and shrugged. He preferred the "empty" air.

"The contest is being held by the fountain," he said, nodding toward a sign next to the mall directory.

"Cool. Let's go—"

"Why don't you two just go on home," a voice interrupted. "I'm gonna win."

Orville didn't have to turn around to know who was speaking—Stu.

"Uh-oh, Stu. You're dangerously close to the vicious Orville volcano," Agatha warned him.

"I'm not afraid of Retardo," Stu said as he passed them, his pace picking up with each step. "I'm just going to get myself a prime place in line." He broke into a jog, glancing back over his shoulder.

"He *is* afraid. That is so delicious," Agatha said as they followed him. "I wonder if anyone else from school is going to show up."

They turned the corner, and Orville saw a line of kids stretching from the fountain all the way to the shoe store at the far end of the mall. He did a scan for sandy-haired boys with good posture, hoping there was an abnormally large sampling. Logically, he knew that he should want to win the contest. It would help them solve the case and clear his mother's name. But his body wasn't responding to logic. His anxiety symptoms were up thirty-nine percent from the moment he and

Agatha had first discussed the possibility of auditioning. He did his best to ignore the sensations as he and Agatha walked down the line to take their place at the end.

"There are a lot of Placid kids here," Agatha observed. "Do you think their parents hired acting coaches for them? Because I have to say, that would be so unjust." She waved to Tim Gore.

"Wright and Wong! Wright and Wong!" the Marshall brothers chanted as Agatha and Orville passed them. Orville cringed. The Marshall brothers were so *loud*. They did the chant every time they saw Agatha and Orville together.

Agatha said it was to show their gratitude for solving the case of the big halftime prank, the one that had ended with the Albert L. Placid field house getting burned to the ground.

If Orville and Agatha hadn't solved the case, the football team wouldn't have been able to play ever again. Agatha said Kenneth and Kevin Marshall would die if they couldn't play football, but Orville didn't think that was physiologically likely.

"Hey, boys!" Agatha called out. Then she whispered to Orville, "I can't believe the slabs of beef are going to attempt to act. Kicking, yeah. Tackling a wide receiver, you're darn tootin'. But acting? I just don't see it."

Orville took his place at the end of the line. There

was one person between him and Stu—Chris Pearson. Orville had never heard Chris say he wanted to be an actor either. Approximately seventy-one percent of the words Chris spoke were on two topics—the *Matrix* movies and cracking security systems.

"Want to see me make all the lights in this place go out?" Chris asked, without saying hello. Orville didn't usually notice things like that. But being around Chris made him feel like he was in social skills class, and Miss Eloise's voice kept popping into his head.

"Meet eye, say hi," he reminded Chris.

"Oh, right." Chris looked at Agatha. "Hi." He looked at Orville. "Hi." Then he blew a bubble. "Want to see me make all the lights in this place go out? I can do it with no more than three keystrokes."

"If you turn out the lights, the contest isn't going to happen. And then I might have to find some way to hurt you," Agatha told him.

"Excuse me." A girl who smelled like red licorice interrupted the conversation. Orville noticed that she had chipped dark blue nail polish that was the color of the sky in locations with relatively little atmospheric dust.

"You two will be a pair," the girl said, handing Chris and Stu sheets of paper. "This is the scene that you'll be doing for Ellen Kroeker, director of *The Cadburys*."

"That means my buddy Orville and I will be a pair," Agatha said, taking the sheets of paper out of the girl's hand before she could offer them.

"Eager much?" the girl muttered. She started to head back up the line.

"Wait!" Agatha and Orville's classmate Lissa Roos called. She rushed over with Jack Simmons right behind her. "We need pages too."

"Hi, Abigail. Hey, Orville," Jack said.

Lissa shook her head. "It's Agatha. Ag-a-tha. You should try to remember it since she's one of the two people who saved our school's collective butt."

"That's okay," Agatha answered, her voice about twelve percent higher than usual and her cheeks approximately fifteen percent redder. "I don't mind."

Why was Agatha turning red? Orville wondered. She had told Orville she had a crush on Jack a few months ago. Orville wasn't entirely sure what that meant, but he wondered if it could be related to the redness. A crush always seemed to involve Agatha behaving in an extremely unusual way. At least, unusual for Agatha.

"It's not okay," Jack said. "Why didn't you ever tell me I had your name wrong?"

A flash of movement in the air caught Orville's attention. Somehow a bird had found its way into the mall. He watched it fly, thinking of the article in *Biplane*

Quarterly he had read the week before. It explained that birds had a small group of feathers attached to the alula—which Agatha insisted on calling a bird thumb. The feathers rested on the bird's wing surface and could be raised so there was a space between them and the rest of the wing. The space increased lift and reduced turbulence. The space between the double wings of a biplane did the same thing.

Orville decided that he should add some bird-observing time to his schedule. The Wright brothers had spent a lot of time watching birds in flight. Their observations—

Snap, snap, snap!

Orville blinked, realizing that Agatha was snapping her fingers in front of his face. Sometimes when he was concentrating on something, he completely ignored everything around him. Agatha had come up with finger snaps as a way of getting his attention.

"Orville! We should watch some of the other people do the scene," Agatha said. "It might give us some ideas on the approach we want to take."

Orville's anxiety symptoms had gone down by more than fifty percent while he was thinking about airplanes, but they spiked when he realized they were approximately 9.2 meters from the raised stage that had been erected next to the fountain.

"You're up," the girl with the licorice smell and the

blue nail polish called to the Marshall brothers. They swung themselves onto the stage, ignoring the steps.

"You shouldn't have said that to me! We share the same mother!" Kenneth bellowed, reading from the script.

"A mother who abandoned us both!" Kevin shouted back.

"Ouch. It's like they're calling plays on the field," Agatha said. "Yelling does not make drama."

"So no yelling?" Orville asked.

"Yelling is only one item in the actor's toolbox. Sometimes yelling is good. But you wouldn't try to build a house using only a hammer, would you?"

The answer to Agatha's question was no, but Orville didn't see what that had to do with the task at hand.

Everyone applauded as the Marshalls finished their scene. Agatha nodded toward a woman sitting in front of the stage.

She was dressed all in black and wore her watch with the face on the inside of her wrist.

"That's the director," Agatha said. "And look, she's not writing anything down. The Marshalls don't even have a wisp of hope."

Tim Gore and Rose Thatcher, a girl who was a Placid cheerleader, climbed onto the stage next. They used the stairs.

"Uh-oh," Agatha said when they were three lines

into their scene. "The two of them are good. Look at Rose. She has tears in her eyes. It's like her half brother really did accuse her of forgery when she was purely innocent." Agatha's eyes flicked to the director. "She's taking notes! But it's okay. It's o-kay. I can make myself cry too. I'll just bite the inside of my cheek. I did that once by accident when my bike went over one of the numerous Bottomless Lake potholes, and the tears just popped out of my eyeballs."

The crowd applauded as Tim and Rose finished their scene. Orville couldn't stop thinking about crying. Agatha didn't expect him to cry, did she? He didn't think he could. He had enough trouble smiling—and he had to remind himself to do that, because Miss Eloise said it was important to other people.

Agatha was applauding again. Orville had completely missed one of the scenes. "The director only wrote down one word," Agatha whispered. "And I'd bet my nana that word was *no*."

Stu and Chris took the stage. They were the last pair before Orville and Agatha had to do their scene!

"You shouldn't have said that to me! We share the same mother!" Stu cried. His voice trembled. Orville couldn't decide if it was acting or if Stu was exhibiting anxiety symptoms as well.

"A mother who abandoned us both." Chris threw his

hands in the air. "Forget about our mother. What's really important are the two pills I hold in my hand. Do you want the red pill? Or the blue pill? You have to decide now!"

"No way. He's doing lines from *The Matrix*." Agatha giggled.

"If so, he's not quoting the movie accurately," Orville replied. "The correct line is—"

"I can't work with this!" Stu pointed at Chris. "I demand another partner. This is unacceptable."

"Choose a pill!" Chris cried, shaking Stu by the shoulders. "Choose!"

Stu pushed Chris. Chris pushed back.

The director stood up. "Thank you! Thanks! That's all I need to see!"

"You idiot! You ruined it for me!" Stu yelled.

"Your eyes hurt because you've never used them!" Chris exclaimed. "*The Matrix* rules! Send in your post-cards asking for *The Matrix 4*." He flung a handful of postcards into the crowd, then jumped off the stage. Stu stared after him.

"Thank you," the director said again.

Stu stomped down the stairs.

Then it was Agatha and Orville's turn.

Orville tried to remember what the maximum recorded human heart rate was. He couldn't, and he usually had no problem recalling any piece of data he had read or heard. Was memory loss another anxiety symptom?

"Try to change expressions a couple of times, just to keep things interesting," Agatha whispered. They got into position in front of the director.

"I'm ready when you are," the director called.

Agatha cleared her throat. She gave Orville a look that said, *You can do this*. Then she began.

"You shouldn't have said that to me," she said, her voice not much louder than a whisper. "We share the same mother!" Her voice rose from an estimated forty decibels to an estimated seventy-five.

"A mother who abandoned us both," Orville replied.

Orville saw Agatha's left cheek become concave, and a moment later tears were running down her face. "Yes. She abandoned us both. Doesn't that mean anything to you?"

"No. I'm nothing like you. I never will be," Orville said. He willed his mouth to turn up at the corners so that his expression would change.

The audience applauded.

"Nice," the director told them, making a note on her clipboard. "You two have great chemistry. I liked the way you stayed chilly while she was getting all emotional on you. And that smile at the end. It gave me shivers."

"Orville! You gave her shivers!" Agatha exclaimed

when they climbed off the stage. "You're my hero! You're going to walk away with this thing!"

"Walk away where?" Orville muttered as he sat down on the edge of the fountain.

He knew it was physiologically impossible, but the bones in his knees—he couldn't remember their names—felt like they had turned to gelatin.

Three more pairs of kids did scenes, then the director told the crowd she would need a few minutes to decide on the winner.

Agatha locked her eyes on the woman. "Ellen Kroeker, *Cadburys* director, feel my brain waves," she murmured. "My brain waves are saying Agatha Wong and Orville Wright. You will obey the waves and choose Agatha Wong or Orville Wright."

"Femur, tibia, and patella," Orville said.

"Huh?" Agatha turned away from the director to look at him.

"The bones of the knee," Orville answered. "I had forgotten them."

The director climbed up onto the stage. "I want to thank each and every one of you for entering our contest. I know how scary it can be to get up in front of a bunch of people. I'm scared right now."

Agatha gave a laugh that was twenty-two percent louder and seven percent longer than her usual one.

"And I have to say, there were some very—um—

original performances today." Ellen glanced over at Chris. "That made my decision extra hard. So hard that I couldn't choose just one winner. That's right, I've decided to give *two* actors roles on *The Cadburys*. There was one team I just couldn't bear to split up— Agatha Wong and Orville Wright!"

"Orville!" Agatha screamed. She jumped up and down. "We did it. We're going to be on *The Cadburys*!"

Chapter 4

"I had a dream last night that I was dis—covered and became an international superstar. I was particularly big in France. My name was Natalie von Heffod and I had red hair, but I was still me. You know how it is in dreams." Agatha and Orville pedaled their bikes into downtown Placid, where the cast and crew of *The Cadburys* were set up.

Orville nodded and Agatha continued.

"I have to say, as an international superstar who had a cooler name and long wavy red locks, I never had to get up at five in the morning to go to work." She paused. "Don't you just love being able to say that, Orville? We're going to work. To get fitted for cos—tumes. So we can do our scene with Trey Beck tomor—row. So we can be on TV!"

"I thought our goal was to get evidence of Trey Beck's criminal activities," Orville said.

"Well, of course," Agatha replied quickly. "I mean, stardom aside, we're here to find proof that Trey Beck is a big, bad jewel thief. It's totally worth getting up pre-dawn for."

She glanced over at her friend, realizing that getting

up pre-dawn must have totally capsized his strict a.m. routine. "How're you doing? You feeling okay? And how's your mom? I'm sorry, I should have asked that right away."

"My pulse, skin temperature, and blinking rate are nearer the norm than they were yesterday. And I haven't experienced any memory problems," Orville said. "My mother stayed in her pajamas all day. She said that no one would want to buy a house from a thief. She made popcorn three times during the night. At one-twelve, three oh-five, and three fifty-seven."

Agatha groaned. Not bothering to dress or go to work? Not sleeping and stress eating? Poor Mrs. Wright. And poor Orville.

"It doesn't sound like either of you got much rest," she said.

"Nope," Orville agreed. "Hey, look. There's Rocky Road Road." He stuck out his arm to signal a left turn and swung his bike onto the street. He pulled to a stop in front of the huge parking lot of the Albert L. Placid Center for the Performing Arts.

Agatha stopped her bike next to Orville's and saw a thick chain strung across the entrance to the lot. A man was sitting in a little booth next to it. He wore a security badge on a cord around his neck. Agatha read the guard's name—Frankie Pepper.

"Is this the lot?" Agatha asked. "I mean, I know it's a

parking lot, but is it the lot for *The Cadburys?*" There were about twenty cars inside. The rest of the huge space was filled with a triple row of shiny silver trailers.

"This is where the magic happens," Frankie answered. "The trailers are our base camp, and we've taken over this whole block—all the stores and restaurants. We'll be shooting scenes in most of them while we're here. Are you two hoping for autographs? You can wait—"

"We're not here for autographs. We're going to be on the show!" Agatha interrupted. "We're supposed to report to wardrobe ASAP—Agatha Wong and Orville Wright."

Frankie typed their names into a handheld computer. "Here you are. Okay, what you want to do is go past the cars and head to trailer 11B, last row to the left, all the way in back."

"Groovy," Agatha said. "I can't wait to start making magic myself."

Frankie pulled back the chain, and she and Orville biked across the parking lot and down the row of trailers.

"There's 11B," Orville told her.

They found a bike rack and parked. Orville went through his usual routine to lock his ride up just so. Then they knocked on the trailer door.

A woman with a bracelet made of tiny plastic bananas opened it. "Hello! Are you my new stars?" she asked.

"Absolutely," Agatha answered.

"No," Orville said at the same time.

Agatha winced. "We're stars if you define stars as anyone who gets to speak a line on the show."

The woman laughed. "That's straight out of my dictionary. Everybody's a star unless they tick me off. Come on. Enter my domain. I'm Amanda, by the way."

Amanda ushered Agatha and Orville into the trailer. It was stuffed with clothes and accessories—in boxes, on racks, hanging from the ceiling. Agatha's eyes darted from a tuxedo to a pair of thigh-high vinyl boots to a pair of pajamas with cowboys and Indians on them. Her eyes stopped on a pair of Yanuk jeans in what looked to be exactly her size. Agatha craved those jeans. All of Cousin Serena's fashion magazines said they were the brand to wear if you wanted to be noticed. All the hip young stars wore them. If *she* were in that pair of Yanuks, Jack Simmons couldn't possibly call her Abigail ever again.

"Do I hear violins? Is someone in looove?" Amanda teased, following Agatha's eyes to the pants.

As if something so miraculous could be described by a word as simple as *pants*.

"Yeah," Agatha said. It was all she could get out.

Amanda grabbed the jeans off their hanger and handed them to Agatha. "These could work. You're going to be playing a friend of Lace Cadbury, daughter of ultra-rich Ryan Cadbury, which means that you're a girl who would definitely have an allowance big enough for Yanuks."

"Really? I can wear them?" Agatha hugged the jeans to her chest. She was in heaven!

Then she remembered—they were on set not for designer jeans, but for a case. "Where is Ryan—I mean Trey Beck—anyway?" she asked. "What do us actor types do around here when we're not acting?"

"If you're Trey Beck, you don't set foot out of your trailer." Amanda flicked through the clothes on the nearest rack and handed Agatha a Speed Racer T-shirt to go with her jeans. "He loves that thing. The rest of us live in hotels when we're out on location, like now. But Trey stays in his beloved trailer and uses his assistant for room service."

Oh, bargain-brand jeans! Agatha silently cursed. She and Orville needed to search Trey's trailer for clues. That was going to be a tad complicated if he never left the place.

Amanda turned to Orville. "Your turn. Let's see. . . ."

"That dark brown hoodie," someone said from the doorway.

Agatha turned and saw a girl about her age standing there. She was gorgeous, with huge brown eyes and blond hair down to the middle of her back. "I know I'm not supposed to have an opinion, but he has eyes like buttery caramel corn, and that hoodie would make everyone notice them," the girl cooed.

Buttery caramel corn? Agatha thought. *Orville?* His light brown eyes were very nice, but . . . buttery caramel corn?

"Well, your basic rich boy does always have a few hoodies in his closet," Amanda said. "Especially hoodies that have been artfully pre-distressed by a celebrity designer. So, okay. He can wear it. But I'm breaking my rules here—*again*. I hope you appreciate it. And don't let it spoil you. I don't want any of you growing up to be Treys. He's always trying to tell me what Ryan Cadbury should wear."

"You won the contest at the mall, right?" the blond girl asked, speaking only to Orville.

'That's us," Agatha answered.

The girl stared into Orville's eyes. "I'm Kath Lingenfelter. I play Lace on the show. Anything you want to know, ask me. I've been a Cadbury since I was two."

"Wow," Agatha said. "So you don't even remember life before acting?"

"I didn't have a life before acting," Kath breathed, dramatically sweeping back her hair. "I've never gone to a day of regular school in my life."

She paused, then stepped closer to Orville. "Maybe *you* could tell me what it's like."

"I think I hear violins," Amanda murmured under her breath. She was grinning as she looked at Kath and Orville.

Wait. *Kath and Orville?*

Agatha's mouth dropped open. Thunderbolt! Kath was crushing on her best friend!

And Orville had no idea.

By the time Amanda finished outfitting Orville, Kath had managed to compliment him seven times. This had amusement value for Agatha, but she soon reached the point where pleasure was about to turn to puke.

"It was great to meet you, Kath," she said, stepping in between Orville and his new biggest fan. "We'll see you later."

"Where are you going now, Orville?" Kath asked.

"*We* have to pick up our script pages," Agatha answered as she opened the trailer door.

"I'll take you!" Kath exclaimed, tossing her hair in Orville's direction. He stepped backward to avoid being touched by it. "I told you, I know everything about the show and the set and all that."

Agatha silently fumed. *How are we going to get anything accomplished now that Orville has a stalker? We'll never be able to investigate with Kath on our tail.*

"The production crew is using the bookstore across the street as an office," Kath told them—correction, told *Orville*—as she led them between two trailers. "One of the PAs—that's production assistants—will get your pages for you."

"Morning, sweetie," a woman with a faint British accent called to Kath. The woman was exiting a large trailer, followed by a man wearing a Hawaiian shirt.

"That's Lavender Langer, the most popular actress on the show," Kath filled in. "She gets more fan mail than the rest of us combined. People watch the show just to see what she's going to do next. Come on, you have to meet her."

"Who's the dude behind her?" Agatha asked.

"That's Robert Stank, the head writer." Kath turned to Orville. "You should be extra nice to him. That way, he'll give you more lines."

A writer. That explains it, Agatha thought. No actor could get away with Robert's wrinkly-shirt-and-ponytail look. Or with a last name like Stank. Any actor would change that name pronto.

"Hey, Robert, Lavender! This is Orville. He's the boy who won the contest yesterday. Oh, and this is his friend." Kath led Agatha and Orville over to them.

"His friend who *also* won the contest—named Agatha," Agatha clarified.

"I look at him, and I see a new series regular," Kath continued without a glance at Agatha. "I see the perfect boyfriend for Lace Cadbury. What do you think, Robert, most talented of writers?"

"Please, no more compliments," Robert begged with

a smile. "Every single actor on this show has been telling me how brilliant and deeply talented I am. Trey Beck even said I should consider modeling."

Lavender Langer laughed as she ran her palm over Robert's pink scalp. "I know what you mean. The show needs to kill someone off more often. All the actors have been practically throwing flowers at my feet. Mark brought me a pair of lovebirds, and Trey gave me an Emmy made of white chocolate. They all think I can save them from your pen of doom, Robbie."

"She *is* the most powerful person around the place," Robert told Agatha and Orville. "She's been on the show for seventeen years! Writers, producers, directors—forget it. Our viewers need their daily dose of the beautiful and sometimes evil Camilla Cadbury. If Lavender ever decided to leave . . ." He shook his head. "I refuse to even speak of it."

"It will never happen," Lavender promised him. She pulled a plastic contact lens case out of her purse, then took a partially dissolved breath mint out of her mouth and stuck it in one of the compartments. Agatha felt her nose wrinkle, and she suspected her face was going all anteater-who-accidentally-ate-a-bee.

Lavender noticed the expression. "I don't believe in wasting anything," she explained. "And these mints are too strong to eat all at once."

Agatha nodded, even though she *so* didn't get it.

"Do you know which Cadbury man is going to be taking a dirt nap?" she asked Robert.

"I wouldn't tell you if I did. But I don't. Ellen, the director, and I are still deciding. And we have to get Lavender's advice, of course," Robert answered, winking at the actress.

"Well, I'm off to the set. Good luck with your scene, darlings," Lavender called. She and Robert walked away.

Off to the set . . . That reminded Agatha. The costume designer had made it sound like Trey only left his trailer to act. So that meant the only time she and Orville could toss the place for evidence was when Trey was *on set* filming a scene.

"Hey, Kath," Agatha said as they headed for the production office. "How do you know when the actors are doing their scenes? Orville and I are here today for wardrobe, and we're shooting our scene with Trey tomorrow—but we don't know exactly when. Is there some kind of master schedule or something?"

"Your scene is with Trey and *me*," Kath corrected, making goo-goo eyes at Orville.

"Ummm, cool," Agatha lied. "So . . . the schedule?"

"They send out a shooting schedule every day," Kath answered.

"Do you think you could get me one?" Agatha asked.

"They already passed them all out," Kath said quickly.

Agatha thought for a moment.

"Ow!" she cried, hoping she wasn't overacting. She staggered back a few giant steps and let herself drop to the ground. "Ow! Orville, I stepped on a nail or something. Look at my sneaker and see if you can pull it out."

Kath put her hands on her hips and sighed as Orville hurried over to Agatha and knelt down beside her.

He looked at her foot. "There isn't any—"

"Ask Kath for a shooting schedule," Agatha whispered, interrupting. "For you. Not me. Not us. You."

"She just said that they are all passed out," Orville reminded her.

"Trust me. Just ask her!" Agatha insisted. She shoved herself to her feet.

"Will you get me a shooting schedule?" Orville asked Kath.

"Sure! One sec." Kath darted to the closest trailer, opened the door, and pulled a sheet of paper out of a metal mail tray attached to the back. Then she slammed the door and sashayed back to Orville. "Here you go, sweet thing."

"My name is Orville," he corrected her.

Agatha tilted her head so she could read the schedule. Oh, yeah! Trey Beck was shooting a scene tonight at five. Which meant that in less than eleven hours, his trailer would be empty.

Empty except for the unstoppable crime-solving duo of Wright and Wong, Agatha thought. *We'll be in there finding the proof that will clear Mrs. Wright's name.*

And send Trey Beck to the big house.

Chapter 5

"That's Trey's trailer," Agatha told Orville when they returned to the lot after school. "I bet he's sitting in there with all the stolen jewelry spread out in front of him. I bet he has his shoes off and he's digging his bare little piggies into the pile."

Agatha leaned back against the props trailer and crossed her arms. Staking out Trey's place was totally easy—everybody spent so much time standing around the set waiting that two kids pretending to read their scripts didn't attract any attention at all.

At four forty-eight, the trailer door swung open and Trey's spiky-haired assistant, Rick, rushed out, his arms loaded down with a heap of dirty laundry. "I need more of those monster eyeballs. Those things are outrageous," Agatha heard Trey call after him. "They're like malted milk balls, but a little crunchier and a lot sweeter. Add them to my list of must-have foods."

"Will do!" Rick closed the trailer door with his foot.

"Trey's going to have to leave his little hideout soon," Agatha murmured. "He's scheduled to shoot in the Duck's Breath restaurant at five. It's ten of now."

"More precisely," Orville corrected, "it's eleven of.

But unless he walks much more quickly than the average person, he will need to leave within three minutes to be on time."

Agatha bit her lip. "Trey doesn't seem like the type of guy who cares about being on time. We might be in for a long wait if—"

"Hey, it's my cutie patootie!" came a squeal from behind them. "I didn't think you'd be back here until tomorrow."

Oh, great. Kath.

Agatha threw up her hands. Peachy. Peachy with a cherry on top. Did Orville's stalker have to show up minutes before they planned to enter the thief's lair? Now they were going to have to get rid of her before they could attempt any snoopage.

"You're so sweet, Orville! You wanted to watch me do my big insanity scene," Kath continued. "I'm up right after Trey. He plays my dad, you know. I'm thinking maybe insanity runs in our family and they'll make him go crazy and, like, jump off a roof or something. You know, if he's the Cadbury man they kill off."

"Sounds important. Shouldn't you be rehearsing?" Agatha asked.

"Nah." Kath shrugged, not taking the hint. "I already prepped with my acting coach."

Trey's door clattered open and he came bounding out of the trailer. He glanced around, his gaze skipping over Agatha, Orville, and Kath. He stared at the golf cart parked outside his trailer. "Rick!" he bellowed. "Golf cart!"

Rick came sprinting back from the wardrobe trailer. "Sorry," he gasped. "I just had to drop off the laundry."

"You're going to make me late." Trey frowned as he climbed into the backseat of the cart.

"Never happen, boss. You will definitely be *on time*." Rick hopped behind the wheel and sped off.

"The Duck's Breath restaurant is only a quarter of a mile away," Orville said. "Trey could easily have walked."

"He could easily learn to drive his own golf cart, too," Agatha replied.

"Trey? Drive? No way!" Kath yelped. "He needs to meditate on the ride over so he can get himself in character. We might as well go watch him while we wait for my scene to start. Come on, gorgeous."

Agatha stared at Trey's trailer. His *empty* trailer. This was their only chance to search it!

They needed an anti-stalker plan.

Agatha thought fast. She could tell Kath they were just about to bike back to Bottomless Lake. Then Kath would walk them out of the lot and wave a sad bye-bye to her cutie patootie. Agatha and Orville could ride around the block and head back to Trey's trailer.

But there was no way to give Orville the you-need-to-let-me-lie alert. If Agatha told Kath that they were about to go home, there was a very good chance Orville would correct her. So that plan was a bust.

"Come on," Kath urged.

Agatha's brain whirred, but she couldn't think of any excuse that would get them away.

Glumly she followed Kath and Orville off the lot and over to the restaurant.

Inside the Duck's Breath, Agatha saw that half the tables and chairs had been removed. Cameras and lights and lots of jumbo electric cords replaced them.

"We can sit over there," Kath told Orville. She wove around the cords and sat down in one of the two chairs behind Ellen Kroeker, the director, and Robert Stank, the writer they'd met that morning.

"Don't worry about me," Agatha said. "I'll stand."

Kath ignored her. Orville ignored Kath. Well, not ignored her exactly. He was clearly deep in The Brain—hypnotized, most likely, by all the complex filming equipment surrounding him.

"It's so great that you're here today. I want to know everything about you," Kath said to Orville. "Like I told you, I've been working on *The Cadburys* since I was two. My birthday is January 20, which means my birthstone is the garnet, just in case you need to know for presents. . . ."

Unless Kath started snapping her fingers in Orville's face, he'd be out of commission for a while. And that meant . . . that meant Agatha could get in a little lying without worrying about any truth-spewing from Orville.

Hmmm. Where to begin?

"Kath, it looks like you're getting a zit on your chin," Agatha interrupted—if you could call it interrupting when the other person was basically talking to herself. "You should stage a preemptive strike before it achieves the nasty white top. You want people admiring your acting when Lace starts to lose her mind—not laughing at your pizza face."

"Oh my God. What should I do?" Kath cried, covering her nonexistent blemish with her hand.

"Clove oil, that's what you need," Agatha advised, channeling her nature-girl cousin Veronica. "But you need to mix it with grape seed oil for the best results. There's a great little store that has the oils down on ZZ Top Lane."

There, Agatha thought. Finding and buying the oils should take Kath at least half an hour, even if she ran all the way to ZZ Top Lane.

Kath pulled a cell phone out of her jacket pocket, flipped it open, and hit a speed dial button. "Mom, I need clove oil and grape seed oil. Buy it on ZZ Top Lane. Bring it to the Duck's Breath set." She clicked her phone closed, gave Agatha a quick nod, then continued telling Orville all the "important facts" about herself.

Note to self, Agatha thought. *Actors behave as if they have no feet of their own. They get things fetched.*

She needed another approach. Fast.

Trey's I'm-a-huge-star entrance pulled her away from her thoughts. She watched him stride across the set toward the writer and director with a smile that showed off every ultra-white tooth in his head.

"Robert, baby. Ellen, baby." Trey kissed both of them on the cheek. "Here I am, the hardest-working actor on the show—and the Cadbury man voted 'most kissable' in a recent online poll—ready to give my all for you two geniuses."

"Marvelous," Ellen told Trey. "Now, in the scene you're about to do, Ryan's heart gets shattered. When Carly Daniels breaks up with him, I want everyone watching to sob. I want to see a big salty river running across the country the day this episode airs."

"You got it." Trey walked over to a table for two and sat down across from an actress in a short, short dress. A large, puffy microphone was lowered into place a few feet over their heads.

Agatha thought harder. And harder—

Wait a minute—she had it! An excellent plan.

She unzipped her backpack and felt around inside. Ah, there it was. One undrunk can of Sea Monster Sludge, her favorite chocolately drink, full of lovely, lovely carbonation bubbles.

Shake, shake, shake.

Agatha jiggled the soda can, careful to keep it hidden behind her back.

Then Trey flubbed a line.

Ellen yelled, "Cut!"

That was Agatha's cue. She raised the can to her lips, angling it just slightly toward Kath.

Here goes, she thought. She popped the top, pulling one of Stu Frysley's favorite tricks. Sea Monster Sludge spurted out of the can, spattering across the back of Kath's silk shirt.

"Eeeeee!" Kath shrieked.

"Oh, no!" Agatha burst out, trying to make her voice quiver. "The can must have gotten shaken on the bike ride over. You'd better get over to Amanda's trailer so she can find you something else to wear in your big scene."

Kath gave Agatha an I-would-so-get-you-fired-if-I-didn't-have-a-thing-for-your-best-friend glare. Then she smiled. "Not a problem. Wardrobe always has multiple sets of the stars' costumes." She pulled out the cell phone again and hit one button. "Amanda, I need another shirt for the insanity scene." She flipped the phone closed.

Foiled again, Agatha thought. And she was usually so good at this kind of thing. *Note to self. Pay attention to previous note to self. Actors have no feet.*

"Let's try it again, people," Ellen called. "And Trey, try to remember the line this time."

"Robert," Trey interrupted. "I don't think Ryan

would say something like, 'When you leave, you'll take my soul with you.' Can't I just say, 'I'll miss you'?"

"What? No!" Robert snapped. "We've been through this a million times, Trey. You have to say the words on the page. What's wrong with you? Can't you remember them all? I swear, *monkeys* have better memorization skills than you."

Trey's mouth began opening and closing as if he were a fish on land. He looked stunned by Robert's words.

"Let's go again. Trey, just say what feels right." Ellen gave Robert an apologetic look, then leaned in to whisper, "Otherwise we'll be here till tomorrow."

"No. I can't work now," Trey pouted. "My body is my instrument. And thanks to Robert, my instrument is much too tense to perform." He whipped out his cell phone and hit a button. "Rick, I need my heated eye pack. And my *Sounds of Whales in Love* CD. And my zinc lozenges. *I need them now!*" Trey shrieked the last four words.

"Oh, perfection. The eye pack," Robert moaned.

Ellen shoved her fingers through her hair. "He'll insist on leaving it on for at least twenty minutes, which will completely ruin his eye makeup. When we start up again, his acting will still reek. And the even sadder thing is, that bozo makes three times as much money as I do." She sighed. "I'm definitely going to remember this when it's time to decide which Cadbury man bites the dust."

She turned around. "Kath, honey, you should go on back to the hotel. We're not going to have time to get to your scene until tomorrow."

Oh, yeah! Agatha thought, her smile growing three feet wide. Kath was leaving—and Trey would be on set all night. That meant Agatha and Orville could search Trey's trailer—finally!

"What?" Kath screamed. "I spent all morning working with my acting coach!"

She stood up and stomped toward the door of the restaurant, passing Rick, who was loaded down with Trey de-stressors. "I would have gotten nominated for the insanity scene. And now it's ruined! Ruined!"

One of the crew members quietly closed the door behind Kath. Agatha reached over and snapped her fingers in front of Orville's face. "I hope you were thinking about something stupendous, because you missed quite a show."

"I came up with a plan for a more streamlined glider," he told her. "I should be able to add several seconds to the amount of time I've been able to keep one of my model planes in the air."

"Really? Well, I got to watch several truly excellent hissy fits," Agatha told him. "As you've probably noticed by now, Kath's gone. Which means we can finally do what we came here for."

Orville stood up. Less than five minutes later, he and

Agatha arrived at Trey's trailer. Agatha bounded up the metal steps, grabbed the door handle, and pulled.

"Locked! Oh, no, Orville, it's locked." She groaned.

"And don't look now, but someone's coming," Orville added.

"What?" Agatha took the three steps with one leap, then she and Orville ducked into the shadows along the side of the trailer.

Rick muttered to himself as he passed them by. "Fuzzy slippers. He can't relax without fuzzy slippers. But did he say fuzzy slippers? No!"

"Orville, do you have gum? I need some immediately—or faster," Agatha whispered.

"I can't smell your breath. You only ask for gum when I can smell your breath from a distance of less than three feet," Orville answered.

"This isn't a breath emergency. It's an *actual* emergency." Agatha rooted around in her backpack and found a linty piece of gum that was half out of its wrapper. She peeled it and jammed it into her mouth. Gross. But sometimes you had to make sacrifices in order to catch the bad guy.

Rick climbed the stairs and unlocked the trailer while Agatha chewed furiously. The second he stepped inside, Agatha slipped up to the door. She caught it before it clicked shut, then stuck her gum into the lock.

She and Orville held perfectly still. A moment later,

Rick re-emerged from the trailer with a pair of dark blue fuzzy slippers. His phone rang as he headed back to the set. "The slippers are in my hands, Trey. Soon they will be on your feet. And yes, I'm running." He clicked off the cell and started to jog.

When he was out of sight, Agatha led the way back up to the door. She held her breath as she pulled on the handle. Ah, sweet, chewy goodness! The door opened, stretching the gum out between the latch and the handle. She grabbed hold of the string and pulled it apart. Poor Rick would probably have to fix that later.

Once inside the trailer, Agatha took in the scene. "I can see why Trey never leaves this place. There's a fridge, TV, DVD player, CD player, lots of slippers, a comfy couch, AC, of course, computer. . . ."

"And evidence," Orville put in.

"Yes," Agatha agreed. "Somewhere in this place there has to be evidence that Trey is a robber."

Agatha stepped up to the desk that held Trey's computer and started going through the drawers. The top one held pictures of Trey. The middle one held yet more pictures of Trey.

So wrong in so many ways, Agatha thought.

The bottom drawer was jammed full of fan letters. Agatha promised herself that all Trey's fans would soon know what kind of person he really was. Sneaky. Stupid. Slimy. And slippery.

"Orville, why don't you check the fridge?" Agatha asked. She began patting down the sofa cushions, feeling around for something diamond-ish. "My cousin Billy has a soda can that's not really a soda can. He uses it to hide the really good pieces of Halloween candy."

Agatha made her way along the couch. All the cushions just felt cushiony. She patted down the stack of magazines on the end table. No jewelry-size lumps anywhere.

"The soda cans are all soda cans," Orville reported. "Everything else appears normal too, although Trey does appears to consume unusually large amounts of cheese."

Agatha tried the adjoining room—Trey's bedroom. She opened every drawer and patted down all the pillows and comforters. Nothing.

"Help me shove the sofa away from the wall," Agatha said, rejoining Orville in the main room. "Maybe there's something underneath it."

With a heave, they both shoved the sofa. It jerked forward a few feet.

Agatha got down on her hands and knees to inspect the floor. The only thing underneath the sofa was a patch of carpet slightly darker than the carpet in the rest of the trailer.

A metallic clang started Agatha's heart racing. Someone was on the stairs!

"Put it back!" she whispered. "Someone's coming!"

She and Orville pushed the couch against the wall, then Agatha scanned the trailer for an escape route. Only one door. And three windows. But three windows that didn't open.

They were so totally trapped!

Chapter 6

The bathroom! Agatha hustled inside and motioned for Orville to join her. She pulled the door closed just as the trailer door began to open.

"I have to lie down!" she heard Trey cry. "The whales and the eye pack and the fuzzy slippers aren't enough. Doesn't anyone understand I'm an artist?"

"Stretch out on the couch," Rick said soothingly. "Would you like something to drink?"

"*Colpisca l'acqua leggermente*. With one lime wedge and two cherries. And a curly straw," Trey said. "Did you tell Ellen that I can't shoot with the two locals tomorrow?"

"The two locals. That's us," Agatha whispered.

Orville nodded. He wrapped his arms tightly around himself. Agatha could tell that being in the small bathroom was giving him the freaks. There wasn't really enough room—she was pretty much forced to stand in his no-touching zone.

But there was no way out except right past Rick and Trey.

"Hang on, Orville," she whispered.

"To what?" Orville asked, his eyelids fluttering.

He really did look like he needed to hang on to something. "The towel rack," Agatha suggested.

Orville grabbed onto the towel rack in front of him like it was the last life jacket on the *Titanic*.

Outside the bathroom, Rick and Trey continued their conversation. "I did talk to Ellen, and she wouldn't allow a change in the schedule," Rick said.

"Whaaat?" Trey's voice came out sounding like a police siren. "Did you tell her that I have a mall appearance tomorrow at the time I'm scheduled to shoot? My fans are going to be waiting for me. I won't disappoint them. I can't!"

Agatha inched open the tiny medicine chest. No jewelry. She flipped open the lid of the hamper with her toe. Empty of clothes and jewelry. She sighed. The search of Trey's trailer was complete—a complete and total bust!

"It's okay. I handled it," Rick said, his voice I-see-a-rabid-dog low and soothing. "Lavender is going to make the mall appearance. The fans will be fine. Everyone loves Lav—"

"Nooo! They're expecting me. Me! And is Lavender me? No, she is not," Trey shouted. "The fans will feel ripped off and wronged. I won't do that to them. I won't!"

Agatha didn't believe Trey cared that much about his fans. From what she'd seen, Trey didn't care much about anything but Trey. Something else was making the soap star go all bananas. But what?

Rick murmured . . . something. Agatha leaned forward to press her ear against the door—and her arm brushed against Orville's. He sucked in a long breath. His Adam's apple began jumping up and down in this throat.

"Orville, Orville, sorry, sorry," Agatha whispered.

He was looking at her, but she could tell he wasn't really *seeing* her. He opened his lips. Agatha knew he was about to let out a scream that could be heard in space. She had to stop him. So Agatha did the only thing she could think of—she slapped her hand over Orville's mouth.

Wham! One of Orville's legs jerked out and slammed into the fake glass door of the small shower.

Crash! He pulled loose the flimsy towel rack. It clattered to the floor.

"Ow!" Agatha cried out as Orville's teeth came down into the flesh of her hand. She whipped her hand away, and Orville let loose a sound that was part squeal and part howl.

The bathroom door flung open, and Agatha and Orville tumbled out.

Rick stared at them in amazement. "The stalkers," he said.

Agatha bolted away from her friend. Immediately

Orville downgraded from a full-on screech to a low moan, almost a hum.

"This is the last thing I needed tonight. The very last thing," Trey huffed. "Rick, call the police."

Rick pulled out a cell phone. "I'm sorry, kids. I'm not going to be able to let you go this time." He dialed a nine and a one—then Agatha snatched the phone out of his hand.

"We aren't stalkers," Agatha blurted. "We're the locals. You know, the ones that Trey is supposed to do that scene with. We, we, we—" Agatha's brain sputtered, then came through for her. "We're here because we wanted to tell Trey that we can't shoot tomorrow. We have to . . . to introduce the swimming pig show at The Grotto restaurant. Since we're going to be on *The Cadburys*, we're Bottomless Lake celebs and, like, you know—" Agatha turned to Trey. "When you're a celeb, you have to make appearances. We couldn't say no because my friend's dad—" She nodded at Orville. "He's the pigs' trainer."

Rick took his cell phone back and started to dial again.

"Rick! Stop that!" Trey ordered. "Didn't you hear her? She and her friend are the locals. And they can't perform tomorrow. They have an important commitment. And a commitment can't be ignored, no matter what Ellen Kroeker thinks. Call her and tell her that none of the actors in the scene are available and that she must reschedule the shoot."

"Great. Yeah. Let's reschedule," Agatha told Trey as she backed toward the door of the trailer. "Have your people call our people. Well, have them call us, because we *are* our people." She pushed open the door. "Come on, Orville."

She scrambled down the metal stairs, praying that neither Trey nor Rick would suddenly decide to ask why she and Orville had been hiding in the bathroom. They reached their bikes, and together they caught their breath.

"I—I bit you," Orville said, still looking freaked out. "I'm sorry."

"I'm sorry too," Agatha said. "I made things worse by touching you."

Orville didn't answer. He didn't even tell her how many gazillions of types of bacteria a human bite could transmit. Agatha could see that Orville wasn't quite himself yet. She purposely gave him a wide comfort zone, staying far away from him as they biked off the lot.

"We aren't introducing the pig show," Orville said when he regained himself.

"I just needed a way to get us out of there," Agatha explained. "And I knew that Trey would be happy to have an excuse not to shoot tomorrow—so happy that he wouldn't ask any questions. And I was right. I'm a genius!"

"Most people say genius starts at one hundred and forty or one hundred and forty-five on the Wechsler Intelligence Scale," Orville reminded her.

Agatha breathed a sigh of relief. Clearly her friend had returned to full Orville power. The touching freak-out was a thing of the past.

"You keep telling me that," she said. "But now the two of us have to put our giganto brains together and figure out a plan for tomorrow. Obviously something's going down at the mall. You heard Trey—he went cuckoo for Cocoa Puffs when Rick told him he couldn't go."

"He said he didn't want to disappoint his fans," Orville commented.

Agatha snorted. "He cares more about his little toe than all his fans combined. We need to find out the *real* reason he's so distressed-obsessed about being there."

"The last time he was surrounded by fans, he stole their jewelry," Orville reminded her. "He might be planning to do it again."

"Could be," Agatha agreed.

"But we can't go to the mall tomorrow. You just told Trey we had to be at The Grotto. If he sees us at the mall, he'll know you were lying," Orville said.

"Good point." Agatha pictured the mall, teeming with fans of Trey—otherwise known as *Trey*niacs.

Chances were, he'd be so swamped by the adoring crowd that he wouldn't notice them.

Then again, if they *really* wanted to keep an eye on him, they'd need to be close.

"You're right, we can't let him see us," she said. "Know what that means?"

"Yes. It means we can't go to the mall tomorrow," Orville repeated.

"Wrong! It means that we need to be incognito," Agatha said. "We need to find the two of us some disguises."

Chapter 7

The next afternoon, Orville stood very still and concentrated on keeping his lips together. Agatha's grandmother preferred for him to wait outside her Trixie gift shop, A Monster's Paradise, whenever he came to visit Agatha.

On the rare occasions when he *was* allowed inside, as he had been this afternoon, it was under two conditions: one, he wasn't allowed to touch anything. Two, he wasn't allowed to say anything.

Touching had often led to breaking, which was why Nana Wong insisted on condition one. Orville answering shoppers' questions about Trixie with a list of reasons why the sea monster couldn't exist had led to condition two.

Nana Wong said that most people didn't really believe in Trixie, but that they wouldn't plunk down their hard-earned cash to buy a souvenir of a sea monster that Orville had just proved could not *possibly* live—not now, not in the past, not ever.

Orville's nose began to itch. He pressed his palms against his thighs and ordered himself not to scratch, because scratching involved moving. He focused his attention on Agatha and Nana Wong.

"The Trixie costume holds on to odors, much the way these cowboy boots do," Nana Wong said, holding up one foot and pointing to her red leather boot. "And no one wants to buy a costume that smells unpleasant."

"We're talking about Orville wearing the costume, not Uncle Boonie," Agatha protested. "Orville doesn't produce a stench. He's cleaner than a cat. No one will ever know anybody had the Trixie 5000 on."

Nana Wong shook her head. "No. It's unsanitary."

Orville agreed. He couldn't say that he agreed, because of condition two, but he agreed.

"You're pretty," Agatha told her grandmother. "Did you do something different to your hair?"

Nana Wong shook her finger at Agatha. "Oh, no, missy. That won't fly."

Orville tried to decide exactly what wouldn't fly. If they showed whatever it was to him, he might be able to get it airborne after analyzing its forces of flight— drag, thrust, lift, weight. . . .

"I'm not going to compromise my merchandise so you and Orville can play dress-up," Nana Wong continued.

"We haven't played dress-up in years," Agatha argued. "Except for Halloween, which doesn't count, because that's dressing up for piles and piles of candy. Besides, we have a serious no-fun-involved need for the costume."

"Which is?" Nana Wong asked.

Agatha snuck a glance at Orville. "What if I told you we needed the costume to raise money for charity?"

Nana Wong stared at Agatha for approximately 2.3 seconds. Orville stared too.

"*Are* you telling me that you need the costume for charity?" Nana Wong finally asked.

"Yes. Yes, I am," Agatha answered.

Orville studied Agatha. She wasn't exhibiting any of the symptoms of lying. The bottoms of her ears weren't red, and neither were her cheeks. Her voice wasn't trembling, and her breathing was regular.

"We're going to charge money for pictures with Trixie, and we're going to donate that money to—" Agatha hesitated for approximately 1.3 seconds. "To the Association of Bottomless Lake Firefighters."

"Huh," Nana Wong grunted.

Orville couldn't decide if the "huh" was a sound indicating a negative or a positive response.

"Come on, Nana," Agatha coaxed. "Do it for the firemen. What is it you call them? Big, burly men, out to do good."

Because of condition two, Orville was unable to point out that one-third of Bottomless Lake's volunteer fire department was female, and of the remaining two-thirds, only sixty percent were both big *and* burly.

"Huh," Nana Wong said again. "Look me right in the

eye and tell me that you're going to use my top-of-the-line Trixie costume to earn money for firefighters."

Agatha put her hands on her grandmother's shoulders and leaned forward. "We are going to use your top-of-the-line Trixie costume to earn money for those brave people who risk their lives to rescue children and kitties—*and grannies*—from blazing walls of flame."

"Two hours. That's it," Nana Wong said. "You will have the costume back within two hours, and you will clean it inside and out."

"Done and done," Agatha answered. "Come on, Orville." She led the way to the back room. Orville followed her. Entering and exiting the store were exceptions to condition one, and there was a door in the back room that led outside.

When they finally crossed the store's threshold, Orville was free to speak. "You didn't exhibit any of the signs that indicate lying," he said. "How did you eliminate them when you told Nana Wong we were going to use the costume for charity?"

"I didn't lie. Nana Wong always knows when I'm lying. Always. So it works best to tell the truth. I figure we *can* sell pictures with Trixie to benefit the fire department. All we have to do is sell one and, hey, ho, no lie committed." Agatha smiled. "Now, let's get you Trixified. I figure the only way to get the costume to the Placid mall is if we bike over with you wearing it.

You won't tip over with it on you. But I guarantee tip-page if we try to strap it to our bikes somehow."

"Why do *I* have to be Trixie?" Orville asked.

"We both have to be in disguise so Trey will feel free to do whatever slippery badness he has planned. The Trixie 5000 will fit you better 'cause you're taller. But if you want to be the harem girl—" She pulled a pair of semi-translucent pink pants out of her backpack and waved them at him.

"Okay." Orville picked up the large Trixie head and slid it on. He looked out at Agatha through the mesh that covered the mask's open mouth. "I'll be Trixie."

"It's a good look for you," Agatha said. "Now, left foot up."

It took Agatha three minutes and forty seconds to get the body of the Trixie costume fastened onto Orville. He thought about his new model glider to keep himself from fixating on the fact that Agatha was almost—*almost*—touching him while she was attaching Trixie's various parts. Even if her hands didn't actually make contact, she was well within the no-touching zone.

Perhaps it was the large Trixie head that kept him from freaking out. Being inside it made Orville's breathing slow and regular. He realized that he felt protected and calm.

When she was finally finished with Orville, Agatha

hurried into the employee bathroom. She emerged less than a minute later wearing the harem pants, a T-shirt with a glittery sea monster on the front, a metallic silver wig that appeared to be made of modacrylic fiber, and a pair of sunglasses with lenses four and a half times larger than average. A Polaroid instant camera hung around her wrist. "Let's hit it," Agatha said. "Our two hours are ticking down."

Orville waddled out the back door and over to his bike. He soon realized that waddling was the only sort of forward motion he could maintain in the costume.

"My peripheral vision has been reduced by approximately sixty-four percent," he told Agatha. "The chance of my reaching the Placid mall without an accident is—"

"I'll be your wingman," Agatha promised him. "The kind that protects you in the wild blue yonder. Or in this case, on the plain old cement."

Orville began to pedal. "That's it. Nice and steady," Agatha called from somewhere to his left. "You got a pothole ahead at two o'clock. Or wait. Make that one. Or wait—"

Orville bounced over the pothole—the first of five he hit on the way out of Bottomless Lake. The street smoothed out in Placid, but his pulse had still reached a rate of almost two and a half times its norm for a bike ride of that length by the time he and Agatha reached the Placid mall.

"Did you two get lost?" someone yelled as Agatha locked their bikes to the rack. Orville rotated his head until he could see the yeller through the mesh opening of Trixie's mouth. It was one of the girls who had been in the game room at the Placid party.

"Freaks belong in Bottomless Lake," the girl yelled. "Sea Monsters too."

Agatha snapped a picture. "Thanks. I needed a photo of a talking butt for my scavenger hunt."

The girl tossed her head and strode away. Agatha grinned in triumph. "After you," she said to Orville as she opened one of the frosted glass doors leading into the mall.

He waddled inside. The waddle had become lopsided because one of his Trixie feet had bent at a thirty-five-degree angle during the ride over. Through his Trixie mouth opening, Orville saw a sign announcing Trey's mall appearance. He pointed one of his plastic claws at it.

"I see it," Agatha told him. "We need to get ourselves over to the fountain. Let's do it undercover style." She veered left, and the stage where the auditions had been held came into view. Trey stood in the center of the stage, surrounded by fans. Eighty-seven percent were women, Orville noted.

Through his tiny field of vision, he could see Trey autographing the leg of one of the women's jeans with a black Magic Marker.

"Okay, who wants to support the Dalmatian lovers, the red-helmet wearers, I'm talking about the fearless, the fierce, the fabulous—the firefighters!" Agatha cried out. "Get your photo taken with Bottomless Lake's own mascot. Money goes to the Association of Bottomless Lake Firefighters."

"I want a picture!" Lissa Roos crossed in front of Orville's mouth-slash-eyes.

"Hear that? The eighth-grade president of John Q. wants a photo," Agatha said happily. "Hold up, Trixie!" Orville came to a stop. Agatha circled around in front of him. There was a click and a flash, then Agatha was collecting a dollar for the firefighters.

Orville tilted his head, trying to get Trey Beck back into his teeny-tiny sight line.

A piece of skirt. One high heel. Long hair. Not Trey.

"Who's next?" Agatha cried. "Who else wants a picture with Bottomless Lake's favorite gal, the one, the only— Trixie." She lowered her voice. "Orville, bow. Or no, curtsy."

Orville put one foot behind him—he bent his knees and began to wobble. Another flash, then Orville turned back toward the stage.

A tall woman slipped into his field of vision and disappeared.

Then a small dog in a big purse.

A man's hands on a woman's neck. A gold necklace glittering as it was slipped into a pocket.

Wait a minute. There it was! The chance to gather the proof they needed—the proof that would show that Trey was the thief! He just had to get Agatha to see it.

"I know that somebody else wants a photo with this lovely creature," Agatha called. "Don't be shy. A dollar for a photo with the sweetheart of Bottomless Lake, Miss Trixie. All proceeds go to real, live firefighters!"

"Agatha!" Orville called. He stood on his tiptoes, trying to get Trey in his sights again.

He saw a hand reaching for a bracelet that looked like it was made of gold scales.

"Agatha!" Orville called. "It's happening!"

The hand unfastened the mermaid-shaped clasp.

"I'm talkin' ten thin dimes for a memory that will last a lifetime!" Agatha cried.

Orville saw the bracelet slide into the same pocket as the necklace. Trey's pocket.

"Agatha!" he yelled, louder this time. "It's happening!"

"What's happening?" Agatha asked.

"The thief," Orville called. "He's thieving!"

"Oh. *Oh!*" Agatha cried. She whirled around, facing the stage. The flash on her instant camera went off. "I got it, Orville! I got a picture of the thief in action. There's no way he can wiggle his way out of this one!"

Agatha told herself she should be happy as she unlocked her bike from the rack in front of John Q.

Middle School. Yesterday she and Orville had achieved absolute proof that Trey was their pickpocket. And now that school was over, they were going to go over to his trailer and get a full-on confession—a confession that would prove that Mrs. Wright was completely innocent.

So Agatha should have been happy. And she was. Just not happy-dance happy.

Why? Because even though Trey deserved his comeuppance, she couldn't help thinking that all of this was going to cause a big stink on the lot of *The Cadburys*. When she and Orville exposed Trey for the jewel-snatching poohead he was, Trey would probably get fired. Then, once he was fired, what would happen to the scene he was supposed to shoot with Agatha?

Agatha had a pretty good idea what. It would be trashed. Flushed. Circular-filed. That meant no watch-Agatha-on-TV party. No chance at being discovered. No chance to change her name to something exceedingly cool—and become big in France.

Agatha sighed and told herself again that she should be happy. After all, she was a detective—not a showbiz star.

"Orville!" she called, spotting her friend heading down the walkway toward her.

He refused to cut across the grass, even though it was quicker. Walking on the grass was a no-no in the John Q. handbook. "Want me to unlock your bike for you?"

"He doesn't need a bike!" Kath Lingenfelter was at the curb, poking her head out of the longest limo Agatha had ever seen.

Actually, it was the *only* limo she'd ever seen, at least in person.

The driver—correction, the *chauffeur*—climbed out of the car and opened the back door. "Get in!" Kath cried. "We'll drive you to the lot."

Awesome-schnawsome! Agatha thought. Maybe they'd never be on TV, but at least they could live like stars for a brief, five-minute ride!

Agatha bent to grab up her backpack. Orville slid into the limo next to Kath. And Kath slammed the door closed.

"Hey!" Agatha exclaimed as the chauffeur started back toward the driver's seat.

Orville rolled his window down. "Wait a minute. Agatha needs to come—"

The smoked window of the limo rose again, blocking Orville from sight. Then the sleek, black car pulled away.

Without Agatha.

A long, loud laugh cut through the silence of her humiliation.

Much too long. Way too loud. Agatha gritted her teeth, glanced left, and saw Stu Frysley, grinning like he'd just been told he was going to get an extra birthday that year.

"You got dumped by Retardo!" Stu continued his donkey-like laugh as he pointed at Agatha.

Agatha turned her back on him and knelt down to tie her shoe—even though the double knot was still solid. She fumbled around in her backpack and pulled out her nail file. She thought she felt a hangnail coming on, and just in case she did get on TV, that was something she needed to fix.

She scanned the rack and noticed Stu's screaming green BMX bike parked on the end.

Yep, good thing she had her trusty nail file. For a shining moment, she pictured herself managing—totally by accident—to stab the metal file through the back tire of Stu's bike.

Agatha was sure she'd feel her anger drain away as the air hissed out.

As it was, she'd have to take out her frustration on the ride to Trey's trailer.

Chapter 8

"I will never be a spoiled actor. I will never be a spoiled actor." Agatha repeated it over and over like a mantra as she huffed and puffed up the final stretch of pavement to the lot. "I will *never* be a spoiled actor."

"Hi, Agatha!" Frankie the security guard called cheerfully.

"Hey, Frankie," Agatha gasped. She'd ridden here double time, as if she could somehow catch up with Kath's limo by sheer force of will—and whatever muscles it took to pedal a bike. "Have you seen Orville?"

"Yeah, I think Kath's got him at her trailer." Frankie rolled his eyes. "Second row, big pink koala on the door."

"Thanks." Agatha rode straight to Kath's trailer. She dumped her bike and pounded on the flimsy metal door. Nobody left Agatha Wong flat!

Kath yanked open the door, tears streaming down her face. Orville stood behind her.

"Hey!" Agatha yelled. A few drops of salt water on Kath's cheeks weren't going to stop her from kicking off the long, detailed, you-are-so-very-rude rant she had prepared on the way over.

"You!" Kath yelled even louder. "I want the truth! What's going on between you and Orville?"

Nothing in her rant fit that question. So instead of kicking off, she had to punt. "Huh?" she asked.

"You and Orville," Kath boomed. "What's the deal? What's the story? What's going on?"

"Um . . . nothing," Agatha replied.

"Then why did he scream at me for leaving you behind?" Kath demanded.

"I did not elevate the level of my voice," Orville corrected.

"Yes, you did! It was awful!" Kath's lips curled in a pout, and a fresh batch of tears poured from her eyes.

Even if Agatha hadn't known that Orville was physically incapable of lying, she would have known Kath was full of a certain highly processed sandwich meat. In all their years of best friendship, Agatha had never heard Orville yell.

"I can't believe he could say things like that to me!" Kath boo-hooed on. "We had such a terrible fight. And I think . . . I think . . . we maybe split up!" She broke off into a wail and rushed back inside.

Orville stepped out of the trailer. Agatha looked him over.

Nope, he was the same calm Orville as usual. He hadn't even achieved the first syllable of upset. He hadn't even gotten to the *u*.

"What did you say to her?" Agatha asked.

"When her limousine pulled away from school without you, I pointed out that her behavior to you was rude according to the rules laid out by my social skills teacher," Orville replied. "But my voice remained within its average decibel range."

"I figured," Agatha said.

"Why did Kath lie about it?" he asked.

Agatha sighed. "She wasn't really lying, Orville. She was just being . . . overdramatic."

"What does that mean?"

"If she told me what really happened, it would sound boring," Agatha tried to explain. "So she kind of exaggerated a little."

Orville blinked at her.

"I don't understand it either," Agatha said. "Being an actor obviously makes people monster weird."

"Maybe Miss Eloise will explain it to me later in social skills class," Orville said.

"Speaking of a lack of social skills, don't we need to have a little conversation with Mr. Beck? A conversation with visual aids?" Agatha asked. She patted the pocket of her backpack that held the incriminating photo.

"Yes," Orville answered.

"Okay. Let's go." Agatha led the way through the lot to Trey's big trailer.

No matter how cute he was, Agatha told herself, no matter how pearly white his teeth, *today he was going down!*

Rick blocked the entrance to the trailer. He sat on the steps, studying a script.

"Hi there, assistant to the star. Whatcha doing?" Agatha asked.

"Oh, I have to read Trey's scripts so I can teach him the lines later," Rick said. "Reading gives him a headache. I do the same with books, magazines—everything. Trey has many interests. He's very well-rounded."

"Cool, um, I guess," Agatha replied. "So is Trey here? Can we talk to him?"

Rick looked worried. "I don't know if that's a good idea. He's doing his vocal warm-ups."

"But I don't hear anything," Agatha said.

"Trey believes in doing the vocal stuff meditatively," Rick said. "He *thinks* through the warm-ups."

"Thinking will not change the temperature of his vocal cords," Orville pointed out.

"Right. So he's wasting his time. And he has time to talk to us whether he knows it or not," Agatha said. She reached over Rick's head and knocked on the door.

Trey whipped it open immediately, all alligator-with-ingrown-toenail-faced. Agatha saw the tantrum coming, so she didn't let him get a word out. "Hi! We need to talk. And I mean seriously talk. Like, in private and immediately." She pushed her way past Rick and right into the trailer.

Orville stayed where he was.

"Oh, you need to invite Orville in," Agatha told Trey. She knew he wouldn't break the social rule of not going where you weren't invited.

Trey gazed at her in confusion. Rick just stared in amazement.

"Just say, 'Come on in,'" she ordered Trey. "Pretend he's a vampire."

"Come on in," Trey repeated.

"Thank you," Orville answered. He stepped into the trailer.

"Now tell your spiky-haired gofer to take five," Agatha instructed.

"Um, Rick? Why don't you go get me some coffee," Trey suggested.

Rick jumped up. "Sure thing, Trey." He took off toward the nearest coffee shop.

Agatha pulled the trailer door shut. Trey stared back and forth between her and Orville. He'd shifted from alligator-with-ingrown-toenail to confused-dog-hearing-barking-on-TV.

"Mr. Beck, I have bad news," Agatha said. "You're busted."

"I . . . don't understand," Trey replied.

"Agatha is typically hard to understand. In this case, she means that we know you have been stealing jewelry," Orville translated.

All the blood drained from Trey's face. He collapsed onto the leather couch, his mouth hanging open. "No! I can't believe you caught me," he moaned.

"That's right," Agatha said, trying to sound tough. "We've got proof." She slapped the Polaroid down on the coffee table. "So don't think you're gonna weasel out of it."

Trey rocked back and forth, whimpering a little.

"Is he weaseling?" Orville asked.

"I don't think so," Agatha answered. "But to be honest, I'm not sure *what* he's doing."

In Agatha's experience, hardened criminals weren't supposed to moan. They weren't supposed to whimper. And they absolutely weren't supposed to cave immediately when somebody accused them of a crime. Especially when that somebody wasn't five feet tall or a high school graduate or a badge-carrying law enforcement officer.

But Trey was an actor. Maybe this was some actorish way of trying to get sympathy.

It wasn't gonna work.

"You're going to give back all that jewelry," Agatha said. "And you're going to make a public announcement saying that you're the thief, not Orville's mother."

"I can't! I don't have all the jewelry anymore." Trey groaned. "Oh! I'm lost! I'm done! My career is over!"

"Then why did you do it?" Agatha cried. "Why did you steal? You already had two scoops of every possible thing you could want—and someone to fetch them for you."

"What was your motive?" Orville translated.

"Survival," Trey sobbed. "I don't want to die!"

For the first time Agatha realized what it must be like to be Orville—totally not understanding the behavior of the people around you. Trey put an extra *odd* in *oddball*. And his behavior was . . . well, it was completely illogical.

"What does not wanting to die have to do with stealing jewelry?" Orville asked calmly.

"Look." Trey pulled a stack of letters from his inside jacket pocket. He threw them down on top of the Polaroid. "I'm the victim here!"

Agatha glanced at the letters. They were all on thick white paper, and they were all covered with glued-on cutouts of glossy magazine paper.

"Wait a minute. These look like ransom notes," Agatha said. The cutouts were words chopped from various magazines—just like in the movies. She handed one to Orville.

"'Steal ten pieces of jewelry from your fans at the

mall. You will be in gargantuin trouble if you don't. You will be dead,'" he read.

Agatha gasped. They weren't ransom notes. They were *blackmail* notes! From someone who wanted to kill Trey Beck!

She turned to her best friend. "Orville, this mystery just got a lot more complicated than we thought."

Chapter 9

"It's extortion!" Agatha cried.

Trey stared at her blankly. "What?"

"Extortion," Agatha repeated. "You know, blackmail."

"Is that one of your cousin Serena's SAT words?" Orville asked.

"Yes, and it's also what's happening right here, right now," Agatha said. "This mystery magazine-cutout person is forcing Trey to do something illegal."

"And if he doesn't, they'll kill him?" Orville asked.

"The notes don't mean that. No, no. It's much worse," Trey wailed. "It means they'll kill off my *character*."

"That's not so bad. You'd still be alive," Orville insisted.

"Yes, but my career would be dead!" Trey shouted. "You don't understand the stress I've been under. Everybody wants to know which Cadbury man is going to die—everywhere I turn, I see it on billboards and on TV commercials. It's a gold mine for the show. They don't even care that the whole thing is giving me an ulcer!"

"And making you steal from people," Orville pointed out.

"Yeah, that too," Trey agreed. "It's horrible. I can't

believe someone is willing to kill me off just for a few pieces of gold. Why would anybody want to do such a thing? I have to sit down—I'm hyperventilating. Rick! Paper bag!"

"I'll get it," Agatha said quickly. Rick was out getting coffee. And besides, she didn't want him involved until they'd figured out what to do about this new wrinkle in the clearing-Mrs.-Wright's-name plan. She rummaged around in Trey's kitchenette and came up with a mini–paper bag for him to breathe into.

"It's my whole life," Trey went on, his voice only slightly muffled by the bag. "I've been on this show since I was eighteen. Sure, I do a TV movie here and there, but *The Cadburys* is my bread and butter. It's my home! It made me famous. If they kill me off, I'll be nothing."

He dropped the bag to his side as if he'd become too weak to hold it up to his face.

"How long has this blackmail been going on?" Agatha asked.

"About a month," Trey said. He shuffled through the letters. "This is the first one I got."

It looked very similar to the first note. Same kind of paper. Letters and words cut out of magazines. "'Steal three pieces of jewelry at the press dinner. Real gems and gold only. Or you will be in gargantuin trouble. You will be dead,'" Agatha read aloud. "The blackmailer's gotten greedier. He or she asked for ten pieces in the most recent note," she commented.

"The stress knot in my back has gotten worse every single day since I got that first letter," Trey moaned. "I've had to hire an extra masseuse."

"Yeah, I feel your pain," Agatha lied. "So who do you think it is?"

"What do you mean?" Trey asked.

"Who do you suspect of being the blackmailer?" Orville asked.

Trey just stared at them. Obviously it had never occurred to him to wonder who the perp was.

Agatha sighed. Trey Beck was one of *those* people—people who didn't bother to think about how to get out of a bad situation. It was just like Nana Wong said about Agatha's uncle Boonie: he was a pawn in the hands of fate.

"Have you told your bosses about these notes?" she asked.

"No," Trey said.

"Have you told the police?" Orville asked.

"No," Trey said.

"Have you tried just ignoring them?" Agatha asked. "You know, *not* doing the illegal things they asked?"

Trey looked horrified. "If I don't do it, they'll kill me off. I'll be out of a job."

"You don't know that for sure," Agatha pointed out. "None of the Cadbury men have died yet."

"It's a chance I just can't take," Trey said seriously. "I figure the publicity stunt has got to come to an end soon—they can't keep stringing the viewers along forever. And once a Cadbury man dies and it's not me, then I won't have to listen to the blackmailer any-more."

"But in the meantime you're stealing from people!" Agatha cried. "And Orville's mother is getting blamed. She even lost her job!"

"Agatha and I have solved three mysteries," Orville put in. "There is a chance that we can solve this one too."

"Without getting me killed off?" Trey asked anxiously.

"We can try," Agatha told him. She pulled out her Spider-Man notebook and flipped to an empty page. "We need to make a list of suspects," she said. "Who are your enemies?"

Trey chuckled.

Agatha raised her eyebrows and waited. That always worked for Nana Wong. A few seconds of the Nana look-and-wait and anyone in the world would be singing like an canary.

"I . . . uh . . . I don't have any enemies," Trey finally said. "Everyone loves me."

"Robert wasn't too happy with you the other night, remember?" Agatha asked. "And I don't think Ellen loved the fact that you pulled a hissy and wouldn't fin-ish your scene."

"And Amanda the costume lady told us she didn't

want us to end up spoiled like you," Orville added.

Trey's mouth dropped open. "Robert and Ellen love me. So does Amanda. I'm always giving all three of them fabulous suggestions on scripts and scenes and my wardrobe. I'm an absolute dream to work with!"

Before Agatha could laugh, there was a knock on the door. Rick stuck his head in. "They're calling for you kids on set," he said. "You too, Trey."

By the time they got to the hair-and-makeup trailer, Trey had insulted a food service worker, a guy sweeping the walkway, and the poodle of one of the other actors. Following him was like walking behind Stu Frysley at school—the dirty looks came flying from every direction.

Agatha had a sinking feeling that her suspect list was about to get even longer.

Trey threw open the door of the hair-and-makeup trailer and flung his arms out to the sides. "I'm here!" he cried. "Make me beautiful! Or should I say *more* beautiful?" He laughed at his joke. The hair and makeup people didn't.

Agatha glanced around the trailer. The tiny space was filled with bottles, tubs, and pots of lotion, makeup, and hair products. Four cramped chairs sat in front of four tiny mirrors, all of them surrounded by little lightbulbs.

And Kath Lingenfelter sat in the last chair, wearing

a cat-plotting-to-steal-the-dog's-dinner expression on her face. When Agatha met her eyes, she looked away.

"Come on in and take a seat," a girl wearing a black smock with *Lou* embroidered on it said. She waved Agatha and Orville in.

Trey took the chair closest to the door. Orville went over to the seat next to Kath and sat down. *Gotta hand it to him*, Agatha thought. *He's brave. Brave or he has no clue that Kath is angry with him.*

Kath gave a little *humph* sound and swiveled her chair so that her back was to Orville. He didn't seem to notice.

Lavender Langer squeezed into the chock-full-o'-people trailer. Agatha was sure Orville's skin had moved from crawling to a full-on sprint. "Hey, Sammy. I forgot to take my foil highlighting strips with me," Lavender said.

The hair guy, Sammy, handed over a pile of foil squares. "Thanks," Lavender said. "These are the perfect size to wrap up half a roll. I never eat a whole one when I go out to eat, so I just wrap the rest in one of these."

"The chemicals we use when we do your highlights are pretty strong," Sammy warned.

"Oh, I wash them first. Don't worry. 'Bye now." Lavender swept out of the trailer, all glamorous. Agatha couldn't picture her washing little pieces of foil. Or saving half a dinner roll. Actors were weird.

"All righty. Let's get started." Lou leaned close to Orville, studying his face.

"Um, you can't put makeup on Orville," Agatha told Lou. "He doesn't like to be touched."

Lou nodded. "Okeydokey, I'll just do a little bit. He's so handsome, he doesn't need much anyway."

Kath sniffled loudly. Everyone ignored her.

"No, no. You can't do *any*," Agatha said. "I mean, you can't touch Orville at all. He'll pull a complete freak-out."

"If you touch me, I may be forced to run from the trailer," Orville agreed calmly.

"Well, what about his hair?" Sammy asked.

"My hair is always combed the same way," Orville said. "It can't be changed."

"But kids don't wear their hair like that," Lou argued. "You won't look natural."

"I am a kid and I wear my hair like this. Therefore your conclusion is false," Orville replied.

"You have to have hair and makeup!" Lou cried. "You can't go on camera looking like that. Kath, help me out here."

Kath folded her arms over her chest and stared at herself in the mirror. She didn't answer.

"Don't worry about it, champ," Trey said helpfully. "It's just Lou and Sammy. It's not like actual *people* are going to be touching you."

Lou glared at him. Sammy held the hair scissors tightly, looking like he wanted to attack Trey with them.

Those two do not love Trey, Agatha thought. *Do they not love him enough to blackmail him?*

"You can do whatever you want to me," Agatha offered. "But it's just not gonna happen with Orville."

"If he doesn't have makeup on, the lights on set will totally wash him out," Lou said. "He'll look like a ghost on-screen."

"There's no such thing as ghosts," Orville pointed out.

"It's just one scene," Agatha said helplessly as Sammy circled Orville with a hairbrush. "Does it really matter that much?"

"Yeah. It's not like they're real actors or anything," Trey said. "Come on, let's get going! I've been sitting here for two minutes already. My time is valuable. You don't want to waste it."

Sammy rushed over to the door and yelled for two more makeup artists to come in and help. One of them began styling Trey's already-perfect hair and the other went over to work on Kath. Lou grabbed a case of eye shadow and started on Agatha's makeup. As she worked, she kept shooting disapproving looks at Orville.

Kath spent the whole time staring at Orville too—unless she thought someone else might be looking. Then she stuck her nose in the air and turned away.

Orville sat staring straight ahead the entire time. He was probably thinking about his new model airplane plans. Nobody spoke.

Agatha sighed. Hollywood life was not turning out to be as glam as she'd expected.

When they'd all finished with makeup, Agatha followed Trey out to the set, the Albert L. Placid Diner and Tunes. Rick rushed up with a plastic foam cup of coffee. This was Trey's second one—he had sent the first cup back because it wasn't hot enough.

"Okay, I need you two kids in this booth over here for a lighting check," a tall, thin woman said. She frowned at Orville. "Where's your makeup?"

He blinked at her without answering.

"Um . . . he's going natural for this scene," Agatha explained. "Is it really going to make him look like a ghost?"

"Since ghosts do not exist, it's impossible for anyone to know what they look like," Orville said.

The lighting woman narrowed her eyes and studied him.

"He hates to be touched," Agatha explained. "It's part of his Asperger's syndrome. Putting makeup on Orville would be like trying to give a cat a bath, the kind of cat that has to have one of those 'will bite' stickers on its cage when it goes to the vet."

The woman smiled. "Don't worry about it. You'd be surprised what good lighting can do—he'll look as warm and glowing as a cherub."

"Then why do you always make me look like I have gigantic bags under my eyes?" Trey demanded. "My lighting is much more important than his."

The lighting woman sighed. "I tell you every day—"

"I don't care!" he snapped, getting hysterical. "I want my entire lighting scheme redesigned. Right this instant, or I'm not performing."

The woman bit her lower lip. Agatha knew that she herself did that. Especially when she was trying very hard not to say something she wanted to—something not very nice.

"We can change the lighting for your close-ups," the woman finally replied. "But no amount of soft filter will make you look eighteen again."

"How dare you?" Trey gasped.

"Drink your coffee," Rick cried, just in time to stop Trey from exploding into a full-blown rage-athon. "That always makes you feel better."

Trey took a sip—and immediately spat it out. "Are you trying to ruin me?" he cried. "This is too hot! I almost burned my tongue. How am I supposed to enunciate my words properly with a burned tongue? Take it back!"

"But the first cup wasn't hot enough," Rick began.

"And this one is too hot! How hard is it, really?" Trey threw up his hands. Rick rushed away with the offensive beverage.

"Why doesn't he just wait for the two minutes it would take for the coffee to cool down?" Orville asked.

"Because he's a baby," the lighting woman muttered. "I have never in my life worked with such a spoiled brat."

Ooh. Someone else who isn't feeling the love for Trey, Agatha thought as the woman headed toward the lighting board to make some adjustments. Could *she* be the blackmailer?

"Let's go, people. I want to get this one in two takes," Ellen Kroeker called. "On your marks!" She took a seat on the tall director's chair behind a small bank of monitors. The two camera guys rushed to their seats behind the huge machines, and the lighting and sound people anxiously gathered around.

A bunch of extras took their places in the other booths and behind the counter, making the set look like a real diner in the middle of a lunch rush.

"Where's Kath?" Ellen called. "Someone get Kath to set!"

A second later, Kath stomped over and hurled herself into the booth with Agatha and Orville. They were supposed to be friends of her character, but the scowl she was wearing made it clear that she wanted nothing to do with them.

"And . . . action," Ellen called.

The extras began to move around, pretending to eat and talk to each other. Trey walked in and went over to the counter.

Kath's expression changed immediately from a scowl to a huge smile. "I can't *wait* for Pemberley's party this weekend," she cried, leaning toward Agatha and Orville as if they were her BFFs. "So what are you guys gonna wear?"

Agatha was so startled that she forgot her line for a moment. Kath had completely changed personality in one split second. The girl could really act!

"Um, I think the new wrap skirt Camilla designed will look totally groovy," Agatha said quickly, trying to get into character. "But we shouldn't talk about clothes in front of Cade. Look how bored he is."

They both looked at Orville. His expression was blank, as usual. Agatha grinned. He did look pretty bored.

"We have something more interesting to talk about anyway," Orville said. "Your father just walked in, Lace."

Kath gasped and whirled around to look at Trey. "Dad!" she cried. "What are you doing here? How did you find me?"

"It wasn't easy, Jace," Trey replied, stepping up to their booth.

"Cut!" Ellen yelled. "Trey, your daughter's name is *Lace*, remember? Not Jace."

Trey rolled his eyes. "I know, but what kind of a name is Lace?"

"What kind of a name is Jace?" Kath cried.

"Trey, your character has had a daughter for ten years now. How is it possible that you can't remember her name?" Ellen demanded.

"I only found out for sure that she was my daughter two years ago when we had the paternity test done," Trey argued.

Ellen threw up her hands. "I swear, Trey, if you—" Her words choked off as she struggled to keep her anger under control.

Another suspect for the list, Agatha thought. *Ellen the director does not love Trey.*

"Take two," Ellen called. Everyone went back to their original places. "And . . . action!"

Kath went through her lines again with the same big smile. This time Agatha was expecting it. She hit her cue perfectly. Orville did his line, and then Kath spun to look at Trey.

"Dad!" she cried. "What are you doing here? How did you find me?"

"It wasn't easy," Trey replied, stepping up to their

booth. "You're grounded, young lady. No party for you."

Kath ignored the fact that he hadn't said her name. "Grounded? Why?" she wailed.

Trey stared back at her, his brow furrowed in what he probably thought looked like paternal anger. Agatha chose the name "constipated monkey" for the expression. He held it. The look went on . . . and on. . . .

"Cut!" Ellen yelled. "Trey, what's the problem?"

"I can't remember the next line," he said. "And this whole scene is stupid. Where's the drama?"

Robert Stank came running up, ponytail and script pages flying. "The *drama* is in the fact that you don't have a relationship with your only daughter," he cried. "The *drama* is in—"

"Does he always do this in the middle of scenes?" Agatha asked Kath as the two men continued to argue.

Kath just folded her arms over her chest and glared at Agatha.

"Are you giving *me* the silent treatment too?" Agatha asked, surprised.

"Yes," Kath snapped. "But mostly I'm giving it to Orville."

"You are?" Orville asked. "Why?"

"Because we broke up!" Kath cried. "Duh!"

Orville blinked at her. He didn't reply. Agatha figured

he was probably running through the various possibilities of what Kath could mean by "broke up."

"Orville, this is going to be the hardest mystery we've ever had to solve," Agatha whispered.

"Why?" Orville asked.

"Because I'm starting to think that every single person on this set has a reason to dislike Trey," Agatha said. "Any one of them could be our perp. How are we ever going to narrow it down?"

"Maybe we should use another approach," Orville suggested.

It took three more takes for Trey to get all his lines right. By the time they finished, everyone on the lot was heading over to the craft services area for dinner. Kath stomped off without a backward glance.

"I figured out a new approach," Orville said. "Let's track the blackmailer."

"Sounds good, but how?" Agatha asked.

"Trey has to get the jewelry he steals to the blackmailer," Orville pointed out. "If we found out how—and if we tracked the jewels . . ."

"We could catch the blackmailer red-handed!" Agatha finished. She waggled her eyebrows. "Follow me. We need more information."

Agatha headed to the craft services area, then marched straight to Trey's table. He sat alone, while all the other tables were overflowing with cast and crew members.

Agatha and Orville planted themselves right across from him.

"We have to talk about the blackmailer," Agatha said.

"I'm listening," Trey told them.

"Once you steal the jewelry that the blackmailer tells you to steal, what happens? How do you know when to give it to the blackmailer? Where do you leave it? Have you ever seen anybody pick up the jewelry?"

Trey's face took on what she liked to call a kitten-overcome-by-too-much-catnip expression. He was dazed and obviously overwhelmed by all her hard-hitting investigative questions. Clearly she was going to have to take it one step at a time.

"You steal the stuff. Then what?" she asked Trey.

"The next day I get another note," Trey said. "It tells me where to leave the jewelry. It's always in a public place."

"Does the note tell you when to drop off the jewels?" Orville asked. Trey nodded. "Did you drop off the jewelry that you stole at the mall yesterday?" Agatha asked.

"Not yet. I'm supposed to do it tomorrow," Trey replied glumly. "I have to leave it all under the seat of the purple swan boat in the Albert L. Placid Park at three o'clock."

"That's perfect!" Agatha cried. "This will be a piece of cake. And I mean chocolate fudge cake with delicious gooey icing."

Trey just stared at her. So did Orville.

"You make the drop tomorrow just like the note told you," Agatha instructed Trey. "Orville and I will be there watching you. And then when the blackmailer comes to pick up his booty, Orville and I will be there to catch his sorry blackmailing butt!"

Chapter 10 "I don't understand why we have to keep wearing disguises on this case," Orville said on Friday afternoon. "We've never done that before."

He wiped some perspiration from his brow. The thick sweatshirt that Agatha insisted he wear had already raised his body temperature almost an entire degree.

"There are too many people who could recognize us," Agatha explained. "The blackmailer is on the lot. *We've* been on the lot—a bunch of times." She took a bite of the sandwich she'd gotten at the Albert L. Placid Park snack bar. "It's a risk we just can't . . . risk."

"Not wearing my usual Friday outfit is causing my heart to run at a constantly heightened pace," Orville told her.

"You *are* wearing it," Agatha pointed out. "Under the tracksuit."

She had a point. Agatha had promised him he wouldn't have to break his daily clothing habit. And technically he was still dressed correctly for the day. But the bright green tracksuit and the four heavy gold chains—not to mention the six fake diamond rings and the huge

D pendant that hung around his neck—seemed to negate the comfort of wearing his own clothes underneath.

All physical signs pointed to him feeling anxious.

"Why does this necklace say *D*?" he asked.

"I borrowed it from my cousin Darrell," Agatha said. "*D* is for 'Darrell.' And for 'dork,' as I always tell him. Sometimes I switch it up and say 'doofus' instead of 'dork.' Occasionally I even mix them together. 'Dorkus' kinda rolls off the tongue, don't you think?"

"Why does Darrell want to wear his initial on a chain?" Orville asked.

Agatha shrugged. "Why is the sky blue? Why does the earth turn? Why do tourists appear in Bottomless Lake every summer? Darrell does what his friends do, and right now his stupid friends all wear bling."

Orville waited to see if she would continue. But four seconds went by. That meant she expected a response.

"I have no response," Orville informed her.

Usually he could understand and translate Agatha-speech. But today he was finding it difficult. Maybe because he was uneasy in the bright blue swan boat they had rented. In nature, swans were white or black. They were never bright blue, nor were they ever propelled through the water with oars. Also, he had noticed that the boat listed toward its starboard side at a fifty-two-degree angle. Because of this, the chance of it tipping was increased.

"Why did I have to dye my hair?" Orville asked.

"It's to help disguise you. No one will recognize you with that awesome, jet black hair. And it's not dye—it's just glorified hair spray," Agatha explained. "It'll wash out."

"Why didn't you dye your hair?" Orville asked.

"Because I'm hiding mine another way."

It was true. Agatha had stuffed all of her dark hair into a baseball cap. From the back and the sides, it looked like she had no hair at all. But in front, approximately twelve strands of hair had escaped and were falling into her eyes. Roughly every two minutes, she blew a puff of air up at the strands in an attempt to get them away. So far she had not been successful.

Other than the cap, Agatha's entire disguise was a pair of sunglasses and a white cotton sling around her shoulder. It held her left arm up as if she had been injured. Agatha's fake injury had caused them a great deal of difficulty in rowing the boat out into the lake. She could only use one hand, and Orville had a hard time with the oars. He approved of the orderly rhythm required to row the boat smoothly, but his body couldn't seem to make the movements needed to achieve the proper rhythm. No matter how hard he tried, he was always clumsy.

After rowing in a circle for ten minutes, they had decided to just drift. There was no current in the man-made lake anyway. Orville calculated that they had drifted less than two feet since they'd pulled the oars up out of the water.

"If you had truly broken or sprained your arm, it would have been unwise to take a rowboat out into the middle of a lake like this," Orville pointed out. "If we tipped, you wouldn't be able to swim for shore."

"Huh. I never thought of that," Agatha said. "Do a jewelry check, *por favor*."

Orville lifted the binoculars from his lap and peered through them. The purple swan boat was still tied to the little dock in front of the Albert L. Placid Boathouse. So were the green swan boat and the orange swan boat. But Orville only cared about the purple one. He had been looking at it repeatedly for twenty minutes now, and nothing about the boat had changed. The paper bag filled with jewelry that Trey had placed in the boat was still in the boat, sitting right in the middle of the little bench seat.

"That is a poor choice of drop-off location," Orville said. "Anyone at all could wander by and take the bag or simply rent the boat and take it out into the lake."

Agatha shrugged. "Maybe our blackmailer isn't the sharpest knife in the drawer."

Orville didn't see what knives had to do with the bag of jewels.

"Still no perp?" Agatha asked.

"No," Orville replied.

"So who do you think will show up here?" Agatha asked. "It seems like almost everyone we've met has a motive for hating Trey."

"Yes, but not all of them have the power to carry out the threat in the blackmail note," Orville pointed out.

"Orville, you're a genius!" Agatha cried.

She felt the need to point this out frequently, although Orville didn't think it was a fact he was likely to forget.

"Only a few people get to decide which Cadbury man gets killed off. Our blackmailer has to be one of those people. So who do we have?" Agatha asked.

"Robert Stank will be the one to write the script where someone dies," Orville said. "That makes him a suspect."

"Yeah, he hates Trey," Agatha agreed. "He said a monkey would be a better actor." She thought for a moment. "Lavender Langer is a big kahuna there. I bet if she wanted someone killed off, they would do it. Robert even said that they'd get her advice on which Cadbury man to ax."

"So she has the power," Orville said. "But what's her motive?"

"She's always saving things like mints and rolls and foil squares," Agatha remembered. "Maybe she doesn't have a lot of money. Maybe she needs the jewelry Trey is stealing."

Orville nodded. "And then there's the director—Ellen Kroeker. Trey's tantrums and mistakes make every scene he's in take longer than it should."

"That's right!" Agatha cheered. "She even said she'd remember how difficult he was when they decided who to kill off. So she's got motive *and* she has the power to carry out the threat."

"Now all we have to do is wait and see which one of them it is." Orville lifted the binoculars and checked the purple swan boat again. It looked exactly the same.

Agatha squirmed around, trying to get comfortable without taking her arm out of the sling. "It's really hot."

"Yes," Orville agreed.

Plop! A black liquid droplet fell onto his hand. He glanced up. No overhanging trees, no birds in sight. What could the substance be?

Plop! Another droplet—two seconds later.

"Agatha," Orville asked, "do you know what this—"

"Orville!" Agatha cried, staring at him with her mouth wide open. He could spot the silver filling in her left rear molar. "Your face!"

He was unsure if Agatha was asking him something or telling him something. Regardless, she didn't seem to have finished her sentence. He waited.

"Orville," Agatha burst out. "You have black gunk all over your face."

Three more drops of black liquid fell onto his hand,

along with two drops on his forearm. Orville leaned over the side of the boat and peered at his reflection in the still water. His face appeared to be streaked with dirt.

"It's the black dye hair spray," Agatha wailed. "It's melting in the heat."

Orville felt a trickle of sweat leave his hairline and wend its way down his forehead. "Does this ruin the disguise?" he asked.

"Yes," Agatha said. "And not only that, the dye can burn when it—"

The trickle of sweat made its way over Orville's brow, and a stinging pain shot through his right eye. He didn't hear the rest of Agatha's comment. All of his senses were occupied by the pain. He let go of the oar he was holding and grabbed for his eye.

"Water," Agatha was saying. "Put water in it. Here! I have some bottled."

Orville forced his left eye open and peered at Agatha. She was trying to pour some of her bottled water into a napkin, but the sling around her arm prevented her from holding the bottle at the right angle. She poured the water onto her lap instead.

Orville grabbed the bottom of his sweatshirt and pulled it up toward his face. He had to get the stinging spray out of his eye! His heart rate was extremely high, and his breathing had increased to match it.

He swatted at his face with the edge of the oversized

shirt—and felt the giant *D* pendant smack him, the corner stabbing into his cheek. The rowboat rocked violently.

"Orville, stop moving," Agatha cried. "The boat's going to tip!"

Orville pulled at his shirt with all his strength and managed to get it up over his head. Finally!

Then suddenly the world was sideways.

The last thing he saw was Agatha's wide eyes, her mouth open in a scream. Then the swan boat tipped over entirely. He hit the water.

Remain calm, Orville told himself. His parents had made him take swimming lessons every summer of his life. He was a terrible swimmer, but he had all the rules memorized. He knew just what to do in case of a water emergency. *Breathe out and follow the air bubbles. They will lead you to the surface.*

He opened his eyes. The water was extremely clean and clear. He spotted his air bubbles immediately and tried to swim after them. He swished his arms through the water and tried to kick.

His foot hit the ground. Confused, Orville put his other foot down next to it. Then he stood up. His head broke the surface of the lake.

Agatha stood next to him, her hands on her hips. The sling hung around her neck, empty and water-logged.

"This lake isn't even three feet deep!" she complained. "What kind of stupid lake only comes up to your waist? Our lake is *bottomless*, and they think they're so superior over here in Placid."

"It comes up significantly higher than *your* waist," Orville pointed out as they waded for shore.

"Come on. Let's go check on the jewelry stash." Agatha wrung water out of her T-shirt, then raced over to where the purple boat was still tied up to the dock. The paper bag full of jewelry was gone.

"Nooo!" Agatha cried. "We missed the perp. He was all wrapped up and waiting for us like a big fancy Christmas present and we missed him! It was an open-and-shut case. We were here. He was here—"

"Or she," Orville put in.

"Or she was here. And we missed him!" Agatha moaned. "Or her."

"But the blackmailer did leave a clue." Orville pointed to the floor of the swan boat.

Agatha raised her eyebrow. "What?"

"See that empty bag of peanuts?" Orville asked. "It was not here when Trey dropped off the jewelry. I would have been able to see it from my position in our swan boat. Also, there are peanut shells under your sneaker."

Agatha moved her foot, her sneaker making a squishing sound from all the water in it. Crushed under the rubber sole were two peanut shells.

"So our blackmailer eats peanuts," Agatha said thoughtfully.

"The peanut is one of the most popular nuts in the United States," Orville observed.

"You're right. A lot of people eat peanuts." Agatha slung her wet hair over her shoulder. "But now we know that there's one particular peanut lover who is also a blackmailer. And I have an idea about where that particular peanut lover might go next."

Agatha turned right onto Monster Lane when they entered Bottomless Lake instead of left, which would take them toward home.

"What are we doing?" Orville asked.

"I want to stop at Buried Treasures," Agatha explained. "It's a secondhand shop. If the blackmailer wanted to fence the stolen jewelry, he—or she—might come here to do it."

Orville blinked at her.

"To 'fence' means to sell stolen property," she clarified. "If the blackmailer wants money, he'll sell the stuff to a place like this." She turned the corner and pulled to a stop.

Orville climbed off his bike and glanced around. "My mother says this part of town is off-limits. I'm not supposed to be in off-limits areas."

Agatha pointed to the corner. "Look. Monster Lane

is only ten feet away. You're allowed on Monster Lane."

"But we're not on Monster Lane. We're on Division Street," Orville argued. "I'm not allowed on Division Street."

"That's just a guideline," Agatha said, trying to spin it. "Look—one wall of the building we're going into is actually *on* Monster Lane. And this store is owned by my cousin Alice's boyfriend. It's practically like visiting my family. Your mother would never object to that."

"Your cousin Alice's boyfriend isn't welcome in your grandmother's store," Orville pointed out.

"That's just because he insulted her handmade Trixie mobile," Agatha replied. "And besides, *you're* not really welcome in Nana's store either."

Orville was silent. Agatha knew she had him, at least for the moment. The only way to keep Orville from following rules was to keep him distracted. She had to move fast.

"Come on, let's lock our bikes to this lamppost," she suggested.

"Wait—it's Lavender," Orville said.

Agatha wrinkled her nose. "Um, Orville, are you losing it? This lamppost is totally green."

"No, it's Lavender Langer," Orville said.

"What? Where?" Agatha whipped her head up just in time to see Lavender leaving Buried Treasures and heading for a little red sports car parked on Monster Lane.

She wore an expensive-looking faux fur jacket and carried an even more expensive-looking tiny beaded purse. But she didn't have a Buried Treasures shopping bag or a Buried Treasures plastic bag . . . or a bag of any kind.

"Guess she didn't buy anything," Agatha murmured.

"But maybe she sold something," Orville suggested.

"Like the jewelry she forced Trey to pickpocket at the mall!" Agatha exclaimed. "Looks like we may catch our perp today after all, Orville! Let's go."

She pushed on the revolving door and went into the secondhand shop. Well, that was what Alice's boyfriend, Buford, called it. Nana Wong called it a pawn shop. Alice said it was a little of both.

"Agatha! Where's your shadow?" Buford greeted her from behind the glass counter.

Orville popped out from the revolving door behind her.

"There he is!" Buford grinned. "What brings you here? Looking for some cheap vintage clothes? 'Cause you two are all wet."

"We had a boating accident," Agatha told him.

It was true that Buford's store had an excellent selection of vintage clothes. Unfortunately, the only kind Agatha fit into were from the little kids' department. But maybe she should tell Amanda in wardrobe to check out Buried Treasures before the show left town. "Hey, Buford, is this all the jewelry you have?"

she asked, glancing into the glass case he was leaning on.

"Yep. Got some nice stuff, though," he said.

"Orville, anything look, um, right?" she asked. She leaned closer and whispered, "Look through your giant cranium. Does anything here resemble the jewelry you saw Trey take in the mall?"

"What are you guys looking for?" Buford asked.

"Just a present for Nana Wong," Agatha fibbed. Adults didn't always like it when she and Orville were involved in crime solving, so it was better not to tell them until it was all over.

Orville studied the rings, necklaces, and bracelets in the glass case. "No. None of these are right."

"Well, if you describe what you want, maybe I can tell you if I have anything like it," Buford offered. "I may have a few things I haven't unpacked yet."

"Do you have a Kazto flower ring? Or a watch studded with diamonds? Or a pendant shaped like a clover?" Orville asked.

Buford looked surprised. He probably hadn't been expecting her and Orville to ask for anything so expensive. "Uh . . . no," he said.

"How about a gold bracelet where the chain is made of links that look like gold fish scales and the clasp is in the shape of a mermaid?" Orville asked.

"Well, no, I haven't seen anything like that," Buford replied. "But check out this pin!" He reached under the counter and pulled out a small pin shaped like a cat. "Nana Wong loves cats. It's Austrian crystal and its eyes are made of real emeralds. It belonged to someone famous. I just bought it from her. I can't tell you who, though. I keep all my clients' secrets."

Agatha knew exactly who he was talking about—Lavender Langer. "Is that cat something we're looking for, Orville?" she cried. She couldn't remember the descriptions of the stolen items. But the cat had to be one, right?

"No," Orville answered.

Agatha's heart suddenly felt as soggy as her still-wet sneakers. She'd thought they had the case solved! But Lavender hadn't pawned the stolen jewelry—she had pawned a piece of her own.

"Guess we'll just have to keep looking," she told Buford.

"Oh. Okay." Buford sounded bummed.

"I'll tell Nana you said hi," Agatha promised him. "She'll get over the Trixie mobile thing one of these days."

"Thanks, Agatha," he said.

Once they were back out on the sidewalk, Agatha turned to Orville with a frown. "I was so sure Lavender was our thief."

"She still could be," Orville answered. "We have the descriptions of everything that was stolen in Placid. But the show has been filming in a lot of towns."

"And the cat pin could be from one of those other towns!" Agatha exclaimed. "It would be smart of Lavender to wait and sell the jewelry in a different place than where Trey stole it."

"It would lower the chance of getting caught by maybe seventy-five to eighty percent," Orville agreed.

Agatha used her fingers to comb her wet hair away from her face. "Phew! A hard day's work—and not even one suspect eliminated."

"The soap opera is only shooting in Placid for two more days," Orville said. "And my mother still doesn't have any buyers asking her to show them houses in Placid. Her popcorn consumption has increased exponentially. She's up to five bags per day!"

"Don't worry," Agatha said firmly. "Tomorrow we're gonna get to the bottom of this."

Chapter 11

Orville checked the clock as he tied his left sneaker. He was right on schedule. He and his mother always watched the tape of Friday's episode of *The Cadburys* on Saturday morning at seven thirty, before she went to Placid for the day. His mother always had at least one open house on Saturdays.

He stood up and walked into the living room. His mother was on the couch—as usual. But everything else was wrong. She wasn't wearing one of her six business suits. She was still in her pajamas. Asleep. With a sixty-four-percent-eaten bowl of popcorn resting on her stomach.

"Mom?" Orville said. She let out a tiny snore.

"Mom!" he said more loudly.

She sat up fast, spilling the popcorn onto the floor. "Oh," she said, staring down at the puffy white popcorn and small brown kernels. "Oh."

Usually when his mother—or anyone—spilled anything, she had the Dustbuster out in five seconds or less, depending on the location of the spill. But she didn't move. She just said, "Oh," again.

Orville hurried to the holder on the kitchen wall

where the Dustbuster recharged when it wasn't in use. He rushed back to the living room and vacuumed up the popcorn, returned the Dustbuster to its slot, then rushed back to his mother and sat down on the couch next to her.

The TV screen was blank. She didn't have the remote in her hand. Orville picked the remote up from the coffee table. He clicked on the television, then hit the play button.

The tape of *The Cadburys* didn't start up. There was no tape in the VCR. Orville felt his stomach twist, as though he'd eaten something bad. He'd had his usual chicken breast, creamed corn, and Oreos the night before. And he hadn't yet eaten his breakfast of hard-boiled egg, apple, and slice of American cheese. So it couldn't be that. Something else was upsetting his digestion.

"Where is the tape of *The Cadburys*?" he asked.

"I didn't record it yesterday," his mother answered. "I'm sorry, Orville. I don't think I can watch the show anymore. When I see Trey, it reminds me of . . . of things I don't want to think about."

"Do you want me to lay out your clothes for your open house?" he asked. Orville never laid out his mother's clothes. But when he was younger, she used to put his out every morning. "You wear your green suit with the brown buttons to a large percentage of the open houses you have in the months between January and March. Would you like me to take the suit out of your closet?"

"There's not going to be an open house," his mother said. "No one wants to buy a house from me, so there's no reason to have one." She straightened up a little bit and patted down the section of hair that was sticking out at a thirty-five-degree angle. "But that's nothing for you to worry about."

Orville studied his mother's face. Miss Eloise had once given his social skills class a handout with drawings of a variety of faces with a variety of expressions. Each expression was labeled. It was a tool to help the students evaluate the moods of others.

His mother had told him not to worry. But she herself was worried. Her face matched almost exactly the drawing of the worried person. With some characteristics of the sad person.

Orville sat next to his mother in silence for a long moment. Without their usual viewing of the tape of *The Cadburys*, he wasn't sure what to do. He wished he could put an arm around his mother's shoulders, the way Agatha could. But that just wasn't possible.

Finally Orville decided that what he wanted to do during the hole in his schedule was talk to Agatha. She would agree to meet him earlier than they'd planned.

Then they could find out who was behind the blackmail, and his mom would be back in her business suits
in no time.

"We're going to figure out which one of our three
suspects is the blackmailer," Agatha said as they headed
onto the lot of *The Cadburys*. "I just don't know how."

Orville thought about it. "I finished reading Nana
Wong's favorite crime novel last night," he announced.
"I now know as much about solving crime as you do."

"You mean *Badge of Bravery*? Rock on with your bad
self!" Agatha replied. "I only read half of it. Can you
believe that book was based on a true crime?"

"Yes," Orville answered. "It said right on the cover
that the story was based on a true crime, so I had no
trouble believing it."

"Well, did you learn anything new?" she asked.

"The main detective said that when he hit a snag in
the investigation, he always went back to the beginning," Orville told her. "I suggest we go back to the
beginning of Trey Beck's crimes."

"The blackmail notes," Agatha said. "You know, I
keep saying you're a genius, but you're not. You're a
super-genius."

"There is no such category," Orville said. "And you
are statistically just as likely to call yourself a genius as
you are to call me a genius."

"Right. Overused word. Noted." Agatha led the way over to Trey's trailer and banged on the door. "Let's get back to the beginning."

Rick opened the door. "You can't come in right now," he whispered. "Trey's sleeping."

"Oh, please," Agatha cried. "You're worse than my aunt Susan with her baby twins." She barged right past him. Orville remained where he was. It was impolite to enter a house when you'd been told not to. And the trailers were like little houses, so it followed that it was impolite to enter a trailer when you'd been told not to.

Agatha rarely behaved in a polite manner.

She stomped up to where Trey was lying on the couch. She whipped off one of his fuzzy slippers.

"Help!" Trey yelped, bolting upright. "Slipper attacker!"

"It's okay, it's all right, everything's good," Rick said desperately, running over to lift Trey's eye mask. "It's just the local kids. They don't know the rules."

"Rules are for sheep," Agatha informed him. "Free-thinking people don't just blindly follow rules."

"Miss Eloise says rules are necessary to the proper functioning of a civilized society," Orville chimed in from outside the door.

"Right. Except for Miss Eloise's rules," Agatha corrected herself. She stared at Trey with the kind of expression that she called a "meaningful look." Orville still hadn't figured out how a look could have meaning, and it appeared that Trey hadn't either. He stared at Agatha for a long moment.

"We need to talk," Agatha said finally. "Remember the *project* we're working on? Things have reached a crisis point. Orville and I need your help."

Trey's eyes widened by a fraction of a millimeter. "Oh," he said. "Right. Yeah. Okay. Rick, um—why don't you take a break?"

"Really?" Rick's face broke into a smile. Orville had never seen that expression on him before. "A break? Just for me?"

"Sure," Trey said. "Oh, and get me a chocolate muffin while you're out. Fat free. But with sprinkles."

Rick's smile vanished. "Fine," he grumbled, leaving the trailer.

"Orville, come on in," Trey remembered to say.

Orville stepped inside and shut the door. "Mr. Beck, we need to study the blackmail notes. Every one you've received."

Trey got the notes out of his jacket, which was hanging in the closet. "I thought you were going to catch the blackmailer yesterday at the park," he commented.

"We ran into an unexpected problem," Agatha said. "But we will absolutely solve the case before you leave town. You have our money-back guarantee."

"We don't charge money to solve mysteries," Orville reminded her.

"Right. But if we did, we'd give a money-back guarantee. And so far we wouldn't have had to give any money back, because we've solved every case. And we're going to solve this one, no matter what it takes."

They weren't talking about his mother, but an image of her lying on the couch in her pajamas flashed into Orville's mind. "My mom would also have our money-back guarantee if we had one, wouldn't she?" he asked.

"Absolutely," Agatha answered. "Your mother would have our double-your-money-back, no-questions-asked super-fine guarantee."

Orville nodded, then he spread the notes out on the coffee table.

"What should we look for?" Agatha asked.

"I'm not sure," Orville admitted.

"Maybe you should just do your brain-vacuum thing and suck up as much information as you can," she suggested.

Orville nodded. He studied the notes, then began telling Agatha what he saw. "There are eight notes, four with demands to steal and four with drop-off instructions. They are all on the same kind of paper. I estimate it to be at least twenty-pound paper in an off-white color."

"It looks like ecru to me," Agatha put in. "And that

paper doesn't look like it weighs anywhere near twenty pounds."

"Twenty pounds is what five hundred sheets of the paper weigh. It's a strange measuring system, I agree," Orville answered, then continued. "The words are formed using letters cut from what appear to be magazines—the paper the letters are printed on is glossy in all but one case. Mostly entire words have been cut, but about fifteen percent of the time the words are formed by individual letters cut from different magazines. Or at least from different parts of the same magazine—it would be impossible to tell which without a chemical analysis of the papers and inks." Orville paused for breath, then went on. "In total, there are twenty-one different typefaces represented. The letters and words are glued onto the off-white paper using a type of clear glue. Again, it would be impossible to tell what brand without chemical analysis."

Trey slumped onto the couch, his mouth hanging slack. Agatha yawned. "What else?" she asked.

"The blackmailer threatens death to Trey in each note," Orville continued.

"Oh, and ooh, the word *gargantuan*. It was in both the notes we read. Is it in all of them?" Agatha burst out.

Orville scanned the notes. "It's in five of the notes,

and each time it is spelled wrong, with an *in* instead of an *an*," Orville replied.

"That's it!" Agatha cried. "Stop right there. We've got our clue. *Gargantuan!*"

"I don't understand," Trey said.

"Neither do I," Orville agreed.

"The blackmailer can't spell *gargantuan*," Agatha said. "All we have to do is get all three of our suspects to write that word. If they can spell it, they're off the hook. If they *can't* spell it, they're our perp!"

"That is not a logical conclusion," Orville told her. "It's an uncommon word. It's quite likely that several people would spell it wrong if we were to conduct a random test. Simply misspelling the word is not concrete proof of being the blackmailer."

"Yeah, but spelling it right is pretty good proof of *not* being the blackmailer, isn't it?"

That seemed mostly true, so Orville nodded. "It could help us eliminate a suspect or two," he said.

"Good. Trey, you stay here. We'll go do what we do best," Agatha said.

"Okay. Have you seen my sleep mask?" Trey asked. "I can't nap without it. I'll get wrinkles if I have to squint."

"You should just close the blinds," Agatha said.

"Sunlight is an important source of vitamin D. I have to be able to absorb it into my skin," Trey replied. "Rick! Sleep mask!"

"Your sleep mask is on top of your head," Orville told him.

"Oh! Thanks. You'd make a great assistant," Trey said. "Talk to Rick. He'll tell you how to get into the biz."

Orville followed Agatha out of the trailer as Trey lay back down on the couch. "I don't want to be an assistant," Orville said. "I want to be an aerospace engineer."

"Don't worry, Orville, you'll be good at that too," Agatha assured him. "Now, let's go find Robert. He's a writer. He should know how to spell. So we can eliminate him right away."

"He should be in the main production office—in the bookstore across the street," Orville said.

It took them eight minutes to get there. Robert Stank was at a desk in the back, huddled over a laptop computer. He jumped when they appeared in front of him. "Can I help you two?" he asked.

"Sorry to interrupt," Agatha said. "Are you writing a script?"

"I'm *re*writing a script," Robert answered. "I need to get Trey into a coma for a few days or I'm going to lose my mind. I'm thinking he can wake up with amnesia and then we won't have to worry about him forgetting everything he was ever supposed to know. Like his own daughter's name."

"Amnesia is extremely rare," Orville pointed out.

"Not on TV, kid," Robert said. "What do you think—it's the end of an episode. Camilla opens the door of her mansion to find Ryan on the doorstep. He's bloody, beaten. He tells her he was attacked by a huge guy in the alley. Then he collapses in her arms and slips into a coma."

"Is he going to die?" Orville asked. "Are you planning to kill Trey's character off?"

Robert laughed. "Nice try! I'm not telling who gets killed. But it's a dramatic scene, right?"

"It's so dramatic I got chills just from hearing you describe it," Agatha cried. Her voice was ten percent higher than usual. It was the tone of voice she used when she was telling a fib to a teacher. "So Ryan falls through the door and says that some *gargantuan* dude mugged him?"

"He says it's a huge guy in the alley, but later on we'll find out it was Bradford Cadbury," Robert told her. "Bradford is pretty short. But Ryan wouldn't want to admit that he got beaten up by his little brother."

"Right, because Ryan has too much pride," Agatha agreed. "So that's why he says it was a *gargantuan* man who attacked him."

"And then the local police will be looking for the huge guy based on Ryan's description," Robert cried. "This stuff is gold! You two are really helping me see it."

"And Ryan will be in a coma, so he won't be able to

tell the cops that it wasn't really a *gargantuan* man who jumped him," Agatha said.

"What's with you and that word?" Robert asked.

"It's one of my cousin Serena's SAT words," Agatha answered. "I like it. It's a big, manly word. Good for a mugger. Maybe you can even have them arrest the wrong guy based on the description," Agatha suggested. "Do you have anyone in the cast who's really *gargantuan*?"

"The actor who plays Umberto is at least six-foot four," Orville said. "And the actor who plays Nicolai is approximately six-foot two, as is the actor who plays Lance MacFadden. And Lance has a criminal record already, so he would be a likely suspect."

Agatha and Robert were both staring at him.

"I see we have a big fan here," Robert said.

"Not really. My mother tapes the show every afternoon and watches it every morning, so I have to watch it too," Orville said. "Or at least I used to." Again the image of his mother lying on the couch, still in her pajamas, flashed into his brain.

Agatha coughed loudly. "So you've got lots of *gargantuan* suspects to choose from," she said. "How does Ryan describe it again?"

Robert began to type. "He came out of nowhere . . . in the alley . . . a huge guy," he said as he typed.

"A *gargantuan* guy," Agatha corrected him.

Robert laughed. "Fine. A gargantuan guy."

Orville moved behind Robert so he could watch as the words appeared on the laptop's screen. G-*a-r-g-a-n-t-u-i-n*.

He typed an i, Orville thought. *Not an* a.

"You spelled *gargantuan* wrong," Orville said. Just then, the word changed on the computer screen.

"Really? Good thing someone invented spell-checkers," Robert answered. He chuckled heartily.

"We should get going," Agatha said. "We just wanted to say thank you for letting us be on the show. It's been a lifelong dream of ours."

Orville opened his mouth to correct her. He'd never once had a dream about *The Cadburys*. But Agatha was wiggling her eyebrows at him. It was probably some sort of sign. He closed his mouth again.

"I should be thanking you two," Robert said. "You've been a huge help with this coma idea. You'd make great writers!"

"I want to be an aerospace engineer," Orville replied.

" 'Bye!" Agatha said, hurrying from the room. Orville followed her.

"Robert has not been ruled out as a suspect," he said.

"I know." Agatha twirled a strand of her hair, which she did forty percent of the time when she was thinking about a case. "Well, we still have to try to eliminate Lavender and Ellen. Let's split up—we can get through them faster that way. I'll take Ellen."

"Why?" Orville asked.

"Because Lavender is a flirt," Agatha replied.

Orville waited for more information.

"She's nice to guys. All guys. You're a guy," Agatha added. "It will be easier for you to get her to write the word *gargantuan*."

"I don't know how to accomplish that," Orville said.

But Agatha was already walking away. "You'll think of something," she called to him. "You're a genius, remember?"

As he walked toward the trailers, Orville tried to think of ways to get Lavender to write *gargantuan*. He didn't think he could use the same method on her that Agatha had used on Robert.

"Orville!" Kath rushed out of her trailer as he passed by. "How weird that I ran into you."

"You came out of your trailer as soon as you saw me," he said. "And you didn't run into me. We didn't have anything close to a collision."

"You caught me." Kath stared directly into his eyes and sighed. "I don't know how to say this, but . . . I've been thinking."

She paused, and Orville counted the seconds. If more than four seconds went by, he would have to think of a reply. But Kath began speaking just at the four-second mark.

"I feel so bad about the fight we had. I'd . . . I'd like to make up," she said.

Her voice was a half octave lower than usual and her rate of speaking had slowed. The only other time he'd heard Kath talk like this was when she was acting. Her character, Lace, spoke in a slow, breathy way, just like all the other characters on *The Cadburys*. But why was Kath talking like that now? Was she acting?

"Are you being overdramatic?" he asked, remembering what Agatha had said about Kath.

"No. It's just . . . I know we broke up and all, but I really hope we can still be friends," Kath said. She blinked several times in a row, which was extremely unusual behavior. But Orville saw no reason to point this out to her. *See it doesn't mean say it.*

"You can call me your friend if you want to," he told Kath.

Kath bounced up and down on her toes and smiled. "Great!" she cried in her normal voice. "So we're friends. And I'm gonna prove my friendship by helping you out."

"Helping me out with what?"

"I don't know. What are you doing? Do you need me to swipe you any schedules or help you find a trailer or anything?" Kath asked.

"You can tell me where Lavender Langer's trailer is," Orville said. "I have to get her to write the word *gargantuan*."

"She's not in her trailer," Kath replied. "She's shoot-ing in twenty minutes, so she'll be in hair and makeup. I'll come with you."

"Agatha says Lavender is a flirt. That means she's nice to guys," Orville commented as they walked.

"Not just guys. Lavender flirts with everyone," Kath said. "Watch." She pulled open the door of the hair-and-makeup trailer. Lavender was inside having her hair done by Sammy. "Hi, Lavender," Kath called.

"Kath! Sweetie!" Lavender gave her a big smile and a wave. "How's my favorite child star today?"

"Good, thanks." Kath glanced at Orville. "See? Flirts with everyone," she whispered.

Orville had no idea whether Lavender was flirting or not. He would have to ask Miss Eloise what sort of behavior indicated flirting. Or maybe he should ask Agatha.

Or maybe . . .

"How should I flirt with Lavender?" he asked Kath.

Kath frowned. "Why do you want to flirt with her?"

"It seems like a good way to get her to write down the word *gargantuan*. I can't think of any other way to do it," Orville admitted.

"Oh. That's easy. Do you have any paper?" Kath asked.

"Yes." Orville pulled his three-subject notebook out of the main pocket of his backpack. Kath snatched it out of his hand and went into the trailer. Orville followed her.

"Hey, Lavender, can you sign an autograph for my friend Orville?" Kath asked. "Just make it out to Orville, your most gargantuan fan."

"I am not gargantuan," Orville pointed out. "Nor am I a fan."

Kath laughed, and Lavender joined in. "Hi, cutie," she called to Orville.

"My name is Orville," he replied.

Lavender grabbed a pen and scribbled the autograph on a blank notebook page. "Thanks, Lavender!" Kath said, skipping back over to Orville.

"Thank you," he called. Lavender blew him a kiss.

Orville studied the autograph. It read, *To Orville, my most gargantuin fan. XOXO, Lavender Langer.*

Orville couldn't believe it! Lavender couldn't be eliminated as a suspect either. And time was running out.

Agatha hid behind the tall, wide sound guy and watched her prey, Ellen Kroeker, directing a love scene between two actors. Ellen Kroeker, suspect in a nefarious blackmailing scheme. Ellen Kroeker, who had openly and publicly admitted that Trey was a bozo who made three times as much money as she did. Ellen Kroeker . . .

Who'd been totally nice to Agatha and Orville and had even chosen them to be guest actors on *The Cadburys*.

Agatha sighed. Sometimes this fighting-crime bit got ugly.

No matter. Time to get on with it. She needed a plan. How did you get a director to write down the word *gargantuan*? It wasn't like you could just go up and ask. Not without a really good cover story, anyway.

It came to her in a burst, the fully formed plan. Like a gift from the mystery-solving gods. Agatha grinned. She was ready. Ellen Kroeker would be helpless in the face of her brilliance. Now she just had to wait for a break in filming.

"And . . . cut!" Ellen called. "Hey, Dee? I think Pemberley should be a little happier when Bradford kisses her. Could you try to look less repulsed?"

The actress on set made a face. "He totally had onions for lunch," Dee complained. "I can't get within two feet of him. It's disgusting."

Ellen sighed. "Mark? Is that true?"

"Dee reeked of garlic the last time we had a love scene," the actor replied. "It's only fair."

"I did not!" Dee cried.

"Did too."

"Stop! Both of you go gargle," Ellen ordered. She turned away as they headed over to the makeup people, who were already pouring cups of mouthwash.

"It's like teaching kindergarten," Ellen muttered.

The sound guy chuckled in response.

Aha! It was time to spring the brilliant plan. Agatha stepped out from behind the big dude and pasted a huge smile onto her face. "Hi, Ellen!" she chirped. "I hope I'm not interrupting."

"Not right now. We're having a Hollywood moment," Ellen joked. "You know, with actors being petty and immature."

"Are there any actors who act like normal human beings?" Agatha asked curiously.

"Oh, sure," Ellen said. "Or at least, there are some who are nice and not spoiled. I don't know if they're ever *normal*. Take Lavender. Biggest star on the show and she's always sweet. Never makes a scene. But she reuses *everything*, from Saran Wrap to dental floss, so I wouldn't call her normal. She's a joy to work with, though."

"She reuses dental floss?" Agatha wrinkled her nose.

Ellen took a swig of bottled water. She nodded. "Till it breaks."

"Gross. Is she a cheapskate?" Agatha asked.

"Not really," Ellen answered. "She's just big into the environment. So she reuses things instead of creating more waste. You know, she shops in thrift stores—sells stuff she doesn't need—buys secondhand furniture and things like that. She thinks it makes her earth-friendly and also down-to-earth. She's probably right."

Agatha thought hard. Was Lavender just green, wanting to conserve the earth's resources and all that? Or was she the blackmailer?

"Did you have fun this week?" Ellen asked her. "You and your friend did a great job."

"Oh. Yeah. Thanks." *The plan*, Agatha reminded herself. *Put the plan into effect!* "Um, listen, can I ask you a favor? My English teacher said I could get extra credit if I did some, uh, 'work-study.' And I figure being an actor is work, right? I mean, kind of. So I was technically doing work-study this week. And I could really use the extra credit. Because I sorta bombed on the last reading comprehension test. Not because I couldn't comprehend—I just accidentally forgot to, you know, read the book that she'd assigned."

"What's the favor?" Ellen cut in.

"Right! The favor!" Agatha took a deep breath. "I just need you to write me a note saying that I've been a gargantuan help to you this week. Because you're the boss and all."

"I'm not the only boss," Ellen said. "And although you did a fine acting job, I don't know if that qualifies as *helping* me."

Words! Words usually came flying into Agatha's brain when she needed them. Where were they now? Ellen wasn't supposed to say no. That wasn't part of the brilliant plan!

"However," Ellen went on, "if you help me direct this next take, I'll write you the note." She smiled.

Agatha breathed a huge sigh of relief. "What do I have to do?"

"Just get everyone back to their places and yell action," Ellen said. "You can sit in my chair."

Whoa! So cool! Agatha climbed into the tall chair and looked around. Dee and Mark were back on set and getting into their places.

"Don't look at them," Ellen instructed from beside her. "As the director, you look at the monitor right in front of you. It shows you what the camera sees and what people will see on their televisions."

Agatha looked at the monitor. Dee and Mark stood with their arms around each other, looking totally bored.

"Action!" Agatha called.

The actors lost their bored expressions.

"I can't live without you, Pemberley," Mark-as-Bradford gasped.

"Kiss me, Bradford," Dee-as-Pemberley replied. "Never stop kissing me!"

They smooched. For a long time. They just kept going. Ewww. Agatha wondered how they could breathe. Ellen nudged her in the side.

"Oh! Cut!" Agatha yelled.

Dee and Mark stopped kissing immediately. Dee wiped her mouth.

"Nice work," Ellen said. She pulled a pad from her back pocket and began to write. "What's your teacher's name?"

"Ms. Dooly."

"Dear Ms. Dooly," Ellen said as she wrote. "Agatha helped me direct a scene of the soap opera *The Cadburys* today. She was a tremendous help—"

"Gargantuan," Agatha interrupted. "A gargantuan help."

Ellen shot her a confused look but kept writing. "A gargantuan help to me and has earned her extra credit." She signed it and handed the paper over.

Agatha glanced at it quickly—and saw that *gargantuan* was spelled right. "Yes!" she cried. She was glad that Ellen was no longer a suspect. Because she was cool. And because eliminating a suspect brought them one step closer to clearing Mrs. Wright's name. And Trey's.

The director stared at her.

"I'm just—*really* psyched about the extra credit," Agatha covered.

A few moments later, Agatha met Orville near the entrance to the lot. "Ellen's off the hook," Agatha burst out as soon as she saw him.

"Lavender spelled the word wrong." Orville handed her an autographed piece of notebook paper.

"So Lavender's still a suspect. And Robert Stank is still a suspect," she said. "I guess one out of three isn't bad."

"But what's the next step?" Orville asked. "How do we figure out which of the two suspects left is the blackmailer?"

"I don't know, Orville," Agatha was forced to admit. "I just don't know."

Chapter 12

"Hey, you two. Wanna see something cool?" Rick asked, approaching them from the direction of the production office. He waved a videotape at them. Orville stepped back to make sure the tape didn't enter his no-touching zone.

"What is it?" Agatha asked.

"Dailies," Rick said. "All the takes of the scene you shot with Trey. The editors will take these tapes and edit together the final product."

"So it's us? On film?" Agatha cried. She grabbed the tape from Rick's hand and stared at it. Orville winced. Miss Eloise would not approve of grabbing, but Rick simply nodded. Perhaps he was immune to rudeness because he worked for Trey Beck.

"I'll set you up in Trey's trailer," Rick offered. "He seems to like you guys. He won't mind if you watch with him."

Five minutes later, they were squished on Trey's leather couch with his TV-VCR combo up and running. Actually, only Agatha was squished, because she was making sure to keep herself as far away from Orville as possible. He appreciated it.

Rick had set out three bowls of Trixie eggs on the coffee table. Trey kept grabbing handfuls from all three.

"Ready?" Rick asked.

"Definitely," Agatha said. Trey just nodded. His mouth was full.

Rick pressed play on the remote and then left the trailer. The TV screen went black, then blue, and then their scene began to play. It looked like a normal television scene but with slight differences. A computerized bar ran along the bottom of the screen, playing back various numbers that indicated recording information. And the sound was strange—much quieter than that on a finished show. There was no background music, and the extras in the diner appeared to be eating, drinking, and talking silently. This caused Orville's heart rate to increase. It was not normal. A room of that size, filled with that many people, would create its own level of white noise. To have it be so quiet was extremely unusual and uncomfortable.

"Cut!" yelled a voice from offscreen.

Everyone on the TV screen relaxed. Then the screen went black again.

Agatha grabbed the remote and hit pause. "Did you see that?" she cried. "Orville, wasn't that cool?"

"There was no background noise. It is unnatural," Orville replied.

Agatha's eyebrows drew together. That generally meant she was confused. "Background noise?"

"He's right," Trey said. "The extras all act like they're talking, but they don't really talk. It would make the sound muddy and the main actors would end up having to re-record everything later as voice-overs."

"But the scene feels wrong," Orville insisted.

"The sound people will add background noise later on," Trey explained. "When you see the finished show, it will sound like a normal restaurant."

Orville nodded. That would be more satisfying. He was impressed that Trey understood and had explained the technicalities of making the show realistic. He had come to expect only rude and unacceptable behavior from Trey.

"I don't know what either one of you is talking about," Agatha said. "All I cared about was us. We were acting, Orville! We're on TV!"

"Oh." Orville hadn't noticed them on-screen. He'd been too distracted by the lack of sound.

"Let's watch the next take," Agatha said. "Pay attention." She hit play.

A whiteboard with some digital numbers flashing on it came into view. "Scene thirty-six, take two," a voice said. The digital numbers changed to match the voice and then the whiteboard disappeared.

The scene started over again.

Orville forced himself to ignore the lack of sound. Instead he looked at the numbers running on the bottom of the screen. One set changed constantly. Most likely that number was keeping count of the frames of film used. A second set remained constant, matching the numbers on the whiteboard from before: 36:2. That was clearly a digital marker of the scene and take. The third number was a date and time stamp.

"Cut!" Ellen Kroeker's voice called from offscreen. The actors all relaxed. Ellen and Robert Stank came onto the set and began arguing with Trey.

Agatha hit pause again.

"Well? Did you see us that time, Orville? Wasn't I awesome?" she asked.

Orville blinked at her. He had not noticed them on-screen. He had a feeling that Agatha would not be happy with that answer. But he couldn't worry about her reaction. There was something much more important that she needed to know.

"There is a time and a date stamp on the dailies," he told her.

"So?" Agatha asked.

Orville pointed to the screen. "One of our suspects—Robert Stank—is right there on-screen and there is a time and date stamp to prove his whereabouts at that time. If we can find the dailies for scenes being shot when the jewelry was picked up from the swan boat, we may be able to eliminate another suspect."

Agatha was already on her feet. "Right! All we need are the dailies for scenes being shot between three and four o'clock on Friday. If Lavender is in them, we can prove that she wasn't at the park making the pickup."

"Robert Stank is on film in these dailies too, even though he isn't an actor," Orville pointed out. "It's possible that we'll be able to eliminate him if we watch the dailies shot during the time the jewelry was taken from the boat."

Agatha nodded. "There are only two suspects left. If we can just clear one of them, we'll know who our perp is."

"You're blocking the TV," Trey complained. "I want to watch myself."

"Trey, we're doing all this to help you," Agatha told him. "You should be more grateful."

"I thought we were doing it to clear my mother's name," Orville said.

"Well, yeah," Agatha replied. "Mostly. I mean, mainly. But it will also help Trey." She turned to the actor. "Where can we find the dailies from Friday?"

"They keep all the dailies in the production office."

"Good. Let's go," Agatha said.

Trey stayed where he was.

"We'll need you to ask for the tapes," Agatha said. "They're not going to give out dailies to Orville and me. We don't even work here."

"You can't expect me to go with you right now. I'm watching my dailies," Trey gasped.

Agatha threw up her hands. "Fine. Never mind." She stomped out of the trailer. Orville turned to Trey. "Goodbye," he said. Miss Eloise had taught him that hellos and goodbyes were very important.

"Later," Trey mumbled. He'd already hit play again.

Orville followed Agatha outside. She was pacing back and forth in front of the trailer. "How are we going to scam those dailies?" she muttered.

Orville thought hard. "I think I know. Come with me."

"I want those dailies NOW!" Kath screeched at one of the PAs in the production office. The guy scrambled to a bookshelf filled with videotapes and began looking for the ones from Friday.

Agatha cringed. Even her great-aunt Margaret didn't have a voice as shrill as Kath's.

Kath turned to Orville and Agatha and rolled her eyes. "You have to get tough with the crew sometimes. They're so lazy."

Agatha nodded, even though the crew had seemed totally fine all week. Kath was helping them, so Agatha was going to force herself to be basically decent. After all, how bad could the girl be if she was smart enough to think Orville was crushworthy?

The PA rushed over with three tapes. "We shot a bunch on Friday," he said.

"Fine." Kath grabbed the tapes and turned her back on him. "Where should we watch them?" she asked.

"We're actually doing a little screening party in Trey's trailer," Agatha said. "I'm not sure it has room for all of us."

"Okay. Orville and I can head over there and you can meet us later," Kath suggested.

"No. Agatha and I need to view the dailies together," Orville put in. "And you can't be there."

Kath looked like she'd been slapped.

"It's just a . . . project . . . we're working on for school," Agatha covered quickly. "Orville doesn't want to bore you by making you help us with homework."

"Oh." Kath relaxed a little. "Okay. Thanks."

"We'll see you later," Agatha told her. "Right, Orville? Say goodbye."

Orville looked Kath in the eyes and smiled. "Goodbye," he said, just as his social skills teacher had taught him.

Kath beamed at him. " 'Bye, Orville!"

They practically ran back to Trey's trailer. Agatha was starting to feel as anxious as Orville in a Trixie suit.

If they didn't find their perp today, they'd be out of luck. *The Cadburys* left town tomorrow, taking all the suspects and clues—and Mrs. Wright's reputation—with it.

Trey was gone when they got there, but thanks to Agatha's gum in the lock, the door opened with a little extra pulling. Agatha hurried inside and popped the first tape into the TV-VCR. Orville carefully closed the door behind them.

"We just need to find the afternoon dailies," Agatha said, hitting fast forward on the remote. She scrolled through the entire tape, her eyes on the time and date stamp in the corner. "This is making me dizzy," she complained.

Orville ejected the tape and put in another one. This time he fast-forwarded, staring at the screen. If he felt dizzy, he didn't mention it.

"There." He hit stop and pointed to the TV. "Three o'clock. Exactly the time the blackmailer picked up the jewelry at the lake. We should watch in regular time now to see if Lavender or Robert appear. If they do, they're cleared!"

Agatha leaned forward on the leather couch and stared at the screen. Two actors were doing a scene outside the Placid movie theater. She watched carefully, hoping for any sign of a suspect.

And then . . . perfecto! Lavender came swishing onto

the screen as Camilla Cadbury. She delivered a cutting remark that sent one of the other characters running off in tears.

"It's Lavender. She's in the scene!" Agatha cried happily. "She's off the suspect list. That means we've found our blackmailer. It's Robert! Robert Stank!" She jumped off the couch and did her happy dance.

"We still have no hard evidence against Robert Stank," Orville pointed out.

Agatha hit eject and pulled the tape from the machine. "True. But now that we know he's guilty, finding the evidence will be easy. Let's go return these tapes. And then we'll stake out Mr. Robert Stank, head writer and blackmailer who can't spell."

The mystery-solving gods were on her side again, because she and Orville hadn't even gotten halfway to the production office when Robert Stank appeared in front of them. He was holding a small bowl of salad, and a bread stick stuck out of his shirt pocket.

"It's the future writers and engineers," he greeted them. "Are you two heading for the craft services area?"

"No," Orville replied.

"Well, you should," Robert said. "You won't believe the dessert spread. They've got two entire chocolate mousse cakes. But they're going like gangbusters. You better get over there if you want a piece."

Why are all our suspects so nice? Agatha wondered. How was she supposed to be happy about taking down a guy who was directing her toward chocolate goodness?

"Why don't *you* have a piece?" she asked, trying to get into interrogator mode.

"I can't eat it." Robert made a face. "I'm prone to kidney stones, and chocolate can cause the stones."

"Chocolate increases calcium oxalate levels," Orville put in. "Seventy to eighty percent of kidney stones are made of calcium oxalate. Uric acid, cystine, xanthine, magnesium phosphate, magnesium carbonate, calcium phosphate, and calcium carbonate make up the others."

"Wow. Maybe you should be a doctor," Robert said.

"I want to be an aerospace engineer," Orville replied.

Robert shot Agatha a smile. She didn't allow herself to smile back. Robert was a bad guy. And Orville didn't go around dispensing medical facts to bad guys without a reason.

Orville cleared his throat—loudly. It wasn't the most subtle hint.

"What's up, Orville?" she asked.

"Peanuts increase calcium oxalate levels too," Orville replied.

"Oh," Agatha said. Then it dawned on her. "Ohhh! *Peanuts!*"

Robert stared at them as if they were as peculiar as Trey Beck, but he quickly recovered. "Yeah, peanuts are a no-no for me too. Bummer, huh? No chocolate-nut brownies in my future." He started away.

"Go eat a piece of mousse cake for me," he called over his shoulder. "It'll make me happy knowing that someone is enjoying it."

Agatha watched him go with a sinking feeling of failure.

"If Robert can't eat peanuts, it's highly unlikely that he is the one who picked up the jewelry and left the peanut shells behind," Orville pointed out.

"I know," Agatha said. "But if Lavender was filming and Ellen knows how to spell *gargantuan*, that leaves us with no suspects at all. Orville, what are we going to do?"

Chapter 13

"We must be missing something!" Agatha cried, pacing up and down in the tiny living room of Trey's trailer.

"Is it *Badge of Bravery* time?" Orville asked.

Agatha sighed. "You want to go back to the notes *again?*"

"It's all we've got," Orville stated.

Agatha hated to admit it, but he was right. They spread the notes out on Trey's coffee table. Orville studied the notes, then took a deep breath and began to spew facts. "There are eight notes, four with demands to steal and four with drop-off instructions. They are all on the same kind of paper," he went on. "I estimated it to be at least twenty-pound paper in an off-white color."

"Check, check, check, check, and checkarooni," Agatha said.

"The words are formed using letters cut from what appear to be magazines—the paper the letters are printed on is glossy paper in all but one case," Orville continued.

"Glossy. Like most magazines, right?" Agatha

flopped down on the couch and tapped the pile of magazines on the end table.

"Right," Orville answered. "Mostly, entire words have been cut, but roughly fifteen percent of the time the words are formed by individual letters cut from different magazines. Again, it's possible that they're from different parts of the same magazine—it would be impossible to tell without—"

"Right, right, without scientific analysis," Agatha cut in. Even after all these years, Orville's ability to retain gobs of boring and minute details astonished her. "Do you think it's worth trying to find out what magazines the letters are from? Maybe it would tell us something about the perp—what kind of mags they read? Or maybe we could try to match magazine subscriptions—to our list of zero suspects."

Agatha sighed. She picked up the magazine on the top of the pile. It was a copy of *Suds*. "I bet everybody on the set gets this one. It's all about soaps." She waved it at Orville.

"I would guess the percentage is slightly less than one hundred," Orville said. "But I agree that it would be a high number."

"There's an article about Kath in this issue," Agatha told Orville. She grinned. "Wanna read about your girlfriend?"

"Miss Eloise hasn't covered boyfriend-girlfriend

interaction yet," Orville said. "But I don't think Kath falls into the girlfriend category."

"Well, I want to see what they have to say." Agatha flipped open the magazine—and gasped. "I don't believe it!" she exclaimed.

"What is it?" Orville asked. "Is it something about Kath?"

"No," Agatha said. "It's this." She laid the magazine down on the coffee table, holding it open with one hand. Words had been cut out of the glossy paper, dozens of words.

Orville began reading one of the articles. "Even though Malachai Travis is"—he paused where a word was cut out—"he will be returning to the show as an angel."

Orville looked up. "It's very likely that the missing word is *dead*."

Agatha grabbed the stack of blackmail letters. She flipped through them one by one. "Here!" she cried. The word *dead* appeared in one of the notes. "The way the word is cut out matches the hole in the magazine exactly!"

Agatha and Orville went to work, matching more words from different letters with the holes cut out in the magazine.

"It seems highly likely that the words from the blackmailer's notes came from magazines in Trey's trailer," Orville concluded.

"But he keeps the trailer locked," Agatha said, her words coming faster and faster. "The only one allowed in Trey's trailer is Trey. So that must mean . . . Trey is the blackmailer?"

Orville didn't answer. He stared at the open magazine, his brain clearly working at full power.

Agatha clenched her fists. They were so close to the answer! They had to be able to figure it out now!

"Or maybe it's not *really* him," she spewed. "Maybe he has multiple personalities. And one of his other personalities was blackmailing him because . . . because . . . because it wanted off the show. Maybe one of his personalities hates being an actor."

"Less than one percent of the population is affected by multiple personality disorder," Orville said. "It's more likely that Trey lied to us about being a victim. Although he didn't exhibit any of the usual physical symptoms that go with lying."

"Well, he *is* an actor. He lies for a living," Agatha answered. "Liar or multiple personality—doesn't really matter. What matters is that Trey is our perp. Trey, his very own self. The magazines are in his trailer. He's the only one who has access to them. Case closed, right?"

"But why would Trey fake blackmail notes?" Orville asked. "What would be his motive?"

Agatha shrugged. "He made up that whole blackmail story just to cover up his evil pickpocketing ways."

"But he already had the notes when we confronted him," Orville pointed out. "He didn't know we were on his trail."

"Huh," Agatha said. "Good point. So it must be the multiple-personality thing, right?"

Orville stayed silent again. Agatha forced herself to be quiet and wait for his answer. "Someone else is in this trailer almost as much as Trey is," he finally said.

Judging by the rushing sound in her ears and the alarmingly violent pounding of her heart, Agatha thought maybe her brain actually *had* exploded.

"Rick!" she cried. "Rick! Rick! Rick! He's always around, getting Trey things, doing stuff for him. So much so, I never even noticed him! And didn't Rick say he reads all of Trey's magazines for him? He's the only one who would ever actually open these things. "

"Does Rick have a motive?" Orville asked.

"Rick has the perfect motive. Trey treats him worse than anybody else on the show. Which is truly saying something." Agatha sprang to her feet. "Wouldn't you hate Trey? I mean, if you were his assistant?"

"I'm going to be an aerospace engineer," Orville answered.

"An assistant probably doesn't make much money. If Ellen said she makes a third of what Trey makes, Rick must make, like, a tenth. That would drive me crazy. Rick waits on Trey hand and foot for peanuts."

"The peanuts he left in the boat?" Orville asked.

"I didn't mean actual peanuts. But yeah, I'm sure Rick's salary paid for those very peanuts," Agatha answered. She slapped her forehead. "Why didn't we have Rick on our suspect list from the beginning?"

Orville shrugged. "It's like my Trixie disguise. It was so obvious, we couldn't see it."

"Well, let's go get him," Agatha said. "He'll be on the set with Trey."

"They're shooting at the Albert L. Placid Train Museum," Orville told her.

Agatha and Orville tore over to the Albert L. Placid Train Museum, raced up the stairs, and flung open the double doors. Orville hesitated. But Agatha flew right into the middle of Camilla Cadbury's living room.

Trey, Lavender, and everyone on set gasped in horror.

"I can't take anymore!" Trey exclaimed. "You've ruined the scene!"

Ellen glared at Agatha. "Out of here! Right now!" she yelled, so steamed she forgot to yell, "Cut!" The cameras kept rolling.

"No!" Agatha cried. "I'm staying right here! I have

something to say. And you all need to hear it. It's vital information."

"Nothing is more vital than the scene, sweetie," Lavender chided.

"This is," Agatha shot back. "This is about *real* people, okay?" She turned in a slow half circle until she spotted Rick with a cup of tea in each hand.

"You've been blackmailing Trey," she accused Rick. "You've been making him steal jewelry for you! You forced him to rob his own fans!"

Everybody gasped again.

Splat! Splat! Both of Rick's paper cups of tea hit the floor. Agatha gave him Nana Wong's look-and-wait. He held out for about two seconds.

"I was going to give it back," Rick said softly. "Anonymously."

And . . . confession, Agatha thought, a grin spreading across her face.

"But why, Rick?" Trey asked. "Why would you do that to me?"

Rick just stared at the tea puddles on the floor.

"You got tired of being treated like a walking hunk of dirt by Trey Beck. Am I right?" Agatha asked.

"But that's impossible," Trey protested. "I treat him like a prince!"

Almost everyone in the room groaned their disagreement.

"Okay, I treat him like every other assistant in Hollywood," Trey muttered.

"Not true. And if it was true, not good enough. You're a terrible boss," Rick said. He crossed the living room set and positioned himself in front of Trey. "I wanted to ruin you for the way you treated me. I figured I'd blackmail you, then get a few pictures of you stealing from your fans. That would have been enough to kill your career for good!"

"So what happened?" Orville asked.

Rick shook his head. "I was outside that charity party with a telephoto lens, and I couldn't catch him stealing. I was practically right next to him in the mall, but—he was too fast!"

"My first role was as one of Fagin's boys in *Oliver!*" Trey said proudly. "I learned to be an excellent pickpocket."

"You should have dressed up like Trixie, the Bottomless Lake monster," Agatha told Rick. She pulled the Polaroid of Trey in mid-theft out of her backpack. "Orville and I had no problem getting this." She let Rick take a good long look, then tore the picture up.

"Someone should call the police," Robert said. "Sorry, Rick."

"Should I stop filming now?" the camera guy asked.

"Yes," Ellen cried. "Cut! That's a wrap!"

• • •

"How can I ever thank you two?" Mrs. Wright asked the next evening. "You have single-handedly saved my career and my reputation!"

"Altogether, Agatha and I have four hands," Orville replied.

His mother just smiled and sat down on the couch next to Agatha. "Do you know, I got calls to show three houses in Placid today. Three! And Prudence Doheny called me herself to apologize."

"Sweet," Agatha said. "That's the perfect revenge."

Mrs. Wright frowned. "Oh, I don't want revenge, dear. I just want to be back in the good graces of Placid society."

Agatha sighed. She would never understand the lure of Placid.

"Um, excuse me. It's six o'clock," Orville informed them.

Mrs. Wright grabbed the remote and clicked on the TV to the local news show. On-screen, Rick was being put into a police car in handcuffs while Trey stood to the side wearing the brow-furrowed expression that he thought looked "concerned."

Then the camera cut to Agatha and Orville standing next to Ellen Kroeker and Lavender Langer. The blond reporter flashed her teeth at them in a huge smile.

"Did Orville tell you that the writer and director

were going to kill off Trey's character?" Agatha asked
Mrs. Wright.

"No! Not that beautiful, kind man," Mrs. Wright
exclaimed. "I won't stand for it."

"Don't worry, Mom. He's safe," Orville said. "They
had to kill off Bradford Cadbury instead. "

"Trey's getting a ton of great publicity for returning
the stolen jewelry to his fans," Agatha said. "The show
would have gotten protests from all over the country if
Trey's character had died."

"How did you two ever figure out that Trey Beck's
assistant was plotting against him?" the reporter on TV
asked the on-TV Agatha and Orville.

"We've solved a lot of mysteries in our time," the
on-TV Agatha said into the microphone. "It helps that
my friend Orville here is a genius. Right, Orville?"

"Yes," he said. "I am."

The reporter laughed.

"My hair looks really good," Agatha said excitedly
as the news report continued describing their adven-
ture.

"My hair looks the same as always," Orville added
approvingly.

Agatha sat back with a happy sigh. Wright and Wong
on the news. And in a week, Wright and Wong on *The
Cadburys*. "Check it out, Orville," she said. "In one
short week, we've caught a pickpocket, stopped a

blackmailer, saved Trey Beck's job, and cleared your mom's name. And we still found time to turn into soap stars *and* reality TV stars!"

Orville felt the corners of his mouth curling into a smile. One he didn't have to force. "You can be a reality TV star. I still want to be an aerospace engineer."